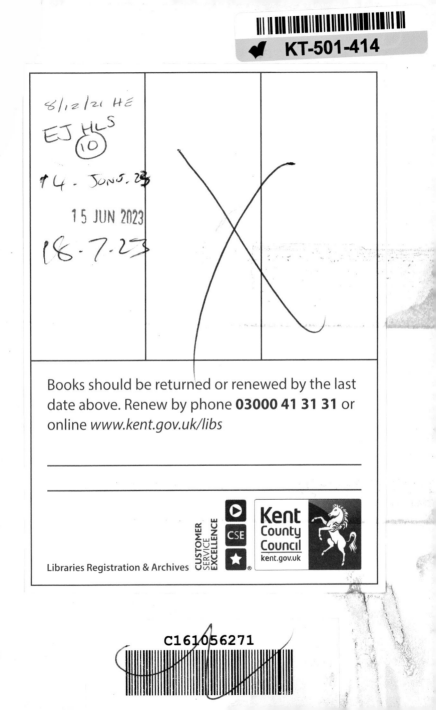

KT-501-414

8/12/21 HE
EJ HLS
(10)
14 - JUN. 23
15 JUN 2023
18.7.23

Books should be returned or renewed by the last
date above. Renew by phone **03000 41 31 31** or
online *www.kent.gov.uk/libs*

TO THE FAR SIERRAS

When drifter Tom Belman's horse is stolen in the Texas panhandle, his pursuit of the young thief leads to an unfriendly reunion with a former soldier in his unit, Lou Currier, now sheriff of the small town of Ortega Point. A subsequent lynching compels Tom to find and return to her home an unknown woman who is also being sought by Currier's posse. But her investigation into the affairs of a local businessman upon returning to Ortega Point will put herself and Belman in grave danger . . .

WILL DuREY

TO THE FAR SIERRAS

Complete and Unabridged

LINFORD
Leicester

First published in Great Britain in 2017 by
Robert Hale
an imprint of The Crowood Press
Wiltshire

First Linford Edition
published 2020
by arrangement with
The Crowood Press
Wiltshire

A catalogue record for this book is available
from the British Library.

ISBN 978–1–4448–4492–4

Published by
Ulverscroft Limited
Anstey, Leicestershire

Set by Words & Graphics Ltd.
Anstey, Leicestershire
Printed and bound in Great Britain by
T. J. International Ltd., Padstow, Cornwall

This book is printed on acid-free paper

1

Lifting his eyes to the horizon had become habitual for Tom Belman. He looked west each morning as he mounted his riding horse, each time he stopped to eat, find shade or tend to the animals, and each night when he halted and undid his bedroll. This night was no different; his gaze slowly swept the terrain while, in the hastening gloom, he unsaddled the horse, then unloaded the packs from the patient mule. It was as though he was committing to memory every landmark; noting the site of every rock, bush and tree that stood between him and that distant point where a sky, still stained pink, touched the ground.

On this occasion, there wasn't much to commit to memory. This territory was flat grassland, interrupted here and there by nature's signposts: small clumps of trees or those great boulders the presence of which in such a place was a complete mystery to him. Sometimes the weather-smoothed stones stood in isolation but usually they were tumbled into centuries-old formations.

Tom had expected to reach the river before nightfall; that had been the gist of the intelligence he'd been given before leaving Ortega Point that morning, but it was probable that old Sam Dack, his informant, had over-estimated the plodding pace of his pack-mule. Now, as he worked at settling the animals, he wondered if he'd made camp too early. It was possible that the river was only another mile or so ahead because this was confusing country where a traveller encountered rivers, people and even settlements unexpectedly. One minute the terrain seemed devoid of anything but grass, then you found yourself on a rise and below might be a lake, tepee homes, or a collection of wood-frame buildings calling itself a town. That was how he'd stumbled upon Ortega Point.

However, when he'd come across this hillock topped with a stand of trees he'd decided to camp for the night. In addition to providing good grazing for the animals it also provided a vantage point and seclusion. Not that he was averse to the company of other people but it paid to be sure of another man's intentions before inviting him to share your campfire. A multitude of dangers faced a man who travelled alone; accidents and illnesses could mean a lingering, pain-filled death or leave him incapable of defending himself against the fangs and claws of foraging wildcats, bears or wolves. He could become lost on the vast prairie or in the mountain ranges and die of thirst or hunger. A traveller could disappear for ever in this wondrously immense, uncharted and empty land, including by the hand of his fellow man. There were ruthless men who would stop at nothing to gain wealth and power and

3

there were others who were violent merely because they enjoyed it: men who would kill for the contents of a coffee pot. Tom could attest to their existence, he'd met such men back when he'd fought in the pitiless war. Not all of them had worn the Confederate grey of the enemy.

But the West and those verdant valleys that lay beyond the far sierras were his destination.

* * *

Just before dawn Tom opened his eyes, unsure whether his sleep had been disturbed by dream or reality. It needed a moment for him to gather his wits, to come to the conclusion that he'd been woken by the sound of a running horse. But the night played tricks on every man and by the time he was in command of his senses the only sound he could hear was the gentle soughing in the surrounding trees. The starless sky was waning grey in anticipation of the rising sun and Tom knew that any attempt to sleep again would be futile.

Later, sitting on his groundsheet with his back against his saddle, he flung the coffee dregs from his tin mug into the small fire he'd built. He'd fed the animals with oats and now they waited contentedly at the picket line, their heads together like friends at a saloon bar. Soon he would load the packs on to the mule and saddle the horse in preparation for another day's travel, but even while that thought occupied his mind he saw the sorrel jerk, pulling against the restraining rope before nervously shuffling and snorting.

Tom was instantly alert, his hand reaching for the rifle that was lying at his side. A voice behind him broke the silence.

'Easy, mister, didn't mean to startle you. Should have made some noise back there to let you know I was around but I guess I needed to know who you were before I made myself known.'

Tom rolled on to his stomach, his rifle in his hands, the saddle briefly providing a defensive wall. The new-comer stepped forward with his arms stretched wide to show that he wasn't holding a weapon although he had a heavy cartridge belt around his waist and a big Remington pistol in a holster on his right hip. He was a slim lad: a youth, perhaps a decade younger than Tom. A curl of dark hair had escaped from the confines of his high-domed Texas hat to rest on his brow.

'I saw the fire glow,' he explained. 'When I got closer I saw the mule and figured you were just someone passing through.'

Tom was curious about the fellow's choice of words, picking up on an implication that the lad had expected him to be someone else, but he couldn't put his finger on anything definite.

'You got a horse?' Tom asked.

'Sure.' The lad indicated behind him, somewhere in the still dying night. It was a tense, nervous gesture, as though he didn't expect to be believed, but Tom let it pass, surmising that each was as wary as the other.

'There's coffee in the pot,' he said.

'Obliged,' said the youth. 'My name's Cal. Cal Tumbrel.'

Tom put the rifle back on the ground.

'Where you heading?' he asked.

'No place in particular.'

The reply wasn't totally unexpected: people were often reluctant to pass out information about themselves, but there had been more to Tom's question than an interest in the young man's travels. If he was familiar with these parts he might be in possession of some useful information about the route ahead.

'If my calculations are correct,' Tom said, 'there should be a river a few miles west of here.'

Cal lifted the cup to his lips but his eyes remained fixed on Tom, as though he thought the comment about the river had been some sort of test.

'There's a river,' he confirmed.

Tom lifted his head as though hoping the stillness of the early morning would carry the smell of the watercourse to him.

'How long will it take me to reach it?'

'Depends how quickly you're travelling,' Cal said unhelpfully.

Again Tom chose to ignore the newcomer's rudeness.

'I've got the mule,' he said. 'He has only one plodding pace.'

Pausing first to make his calculations, Cal said:

'You'll be there before midday.'

Tom was suddenly aware that his horse was acting fidgety again; its ears were pricked and it was lifting its head in sharp jerking movements. Tom recognized the reaction: a smell or sound had caught its attention. A second or two later the mule too registered its interest, turning its head in its usual slow manner, like an old-timer looking for some place to empty his mouth of the juice he'd chewed from a plug of tobacco.

'What is it?' Tom asked, crossing to the animals and rubbing their muzzles to reassure them. Within half a minute the sound reached him too: the unmistakable drumming that was the music of fast-moving horses.

Cal Tumbrel had also heard the sound of the approaching horsemen; his reaction was decisive and unexpected. He kicked at the embers of the fire, spreading them, and stamped on them to extinguish their glow. He removed his jacket and threw it over the ashes to smother the smoke. By the time he'd turned his wide-eyed gaze in Tom's direction his gun was in his hand.

'Quiet,' he hissed and together they peered into the rosy light of morning.

There were five men perhaps quarter of a mile from the hillock. They rode past without sparing it a glance. The leading horse was a big-framed animal with a deep chest and a high-stepping action that suggested it had been bred for speed. Its rider sat tall, back straight and hands held high, emphasizing that

9

his control of the beast was achieved primarily with knees and heels.

The second rider, half a length behind, was bareheaded, his hat jouncing on his back and his long hair straggling behind with each stretching stride of his galloping cayuse. Even though the light was faint Tom was able to tell that this man was as rangy as the horse he sat astride. There was a restlessness about his movements that was in complete contrast to the rigid riding style of the leader.

The other three riders were almost in a line; their low broncs were struggling to maintain the pace of the two horses in front of them but their riders were persevering doggedly, relying upon the stamina of their mounts to complete the run. Like Tom, the group was heading west, but with a determination and disregard for the welfare of their animals that implied they didn't expect to travel far.

By the time those observations had been stored in Tom's brain Cal had gathered up his jacket. Surreptitiously he kicked Tom's rifle towards some bushes; it was followed by Tom's holster belt and handgun.

'Hey!' yelled Tom.

'I'm taking your horse,' Cal said, pointing the Remington at Tom's midriff to make it clear that argument was useless.

'Are those men looking for you?' Tom asked, and in that moment he recalled an incident that had played out in Ortega Point shortly before his departure from the little town.

* * *

Sam Dack, who was willing to earn a dollar by undertaking any task that wasn't covered by the legitimate tradesmen of Ortega Point, had stabled Tom's animals for the three nights he'd remained in the town. Tom had reached the barn that morning to find the sorrel saddled and the mule expertly packed so that the load was evenly distributed. Within moments a hullabaloo erupted from further down the street. Horses were running, men were shouting and, as the onrushing animals sped past the place where Tom and Sam were standing, a couple of pistol shots cracked to ineffectual purpose.

Although all the running horses were saddled, their reins flying and stirrups swinging, Tom's first impression had been that all were riderless, but then, as they passed and reached the corner of the street, it seemed that they were being driven forward by a figure who was lying low on the rear animal. For a moment, before the horses raced around the last buildings, which took them out of sight and on to the open rangeland, he had thought there might be a second person clinging like a rodeo rider to the side of one of the other animals.

'What's happening?' Sam had asked one of the men who were following the stampede, a man with a star on his chest and a smoking gun in his hand.

'Jail break,' the deputy replied as he made a grab for Tom's sorrel.

'Who did you have locked up?' Sam's voice sounded weighted with surprise, as though the cells in the town jail had never before been put to use.

The man didn't answer the question because Tom's intervention, a restraining hand that prevented him from mounting the sorrel, had become a more pressing problem.

'I'm a deputy in this town,' he exclaimed, slapping the metal badge on his chest to emphasize the point.

'Doesn't give you the authority to take my horse. He's got a long journey ahead. I won't be able to leave town if you race him all over the country — and you'll have to pay my hotel bills for another three-day stay.'

The man was going to argue but another deputy arrived to stress the need for them to get word to the sheriff or Mr Willis.

'Who did you have in jail?' Sam Dack

asked again and again his question was ignored.

Deciding that the incident was none of his concern Tom mounted up and left Ortega Point behind him.

★ ★ ★

'It was you who broke out of the Ortega Point jail yesterday morning,' declared Tom.

'It's not your concern.'

'It is if you take my horse.'

'Just saddle it and you won't come to any harm.' Cal gestured with the big pistol to emphasize his urgency.

'You can't steal my horse.'

'You've got the mule,' Cal remarked, as though they were partners bargaining for equal shares of their property.

'You're not taking my horse,' Tom told him again. 'You said your own was back there.'

'It is. It's dead. I've got to get to the ferry. Fast. Perhaps I'll leave yours there.'

Cal gestured again with the gun he was holding.

Tom wasn't sure he would use it; his visitor had been anxious enough to avoid detection when the horsemen had ridden by, so it seemed unlikely that he would now betray his location. But Tom couldn't be sure. He figured it made more sense to obey for the moment; perhaps there would be an opportunity to turn the tables later. One off-guard moment might be all he'd need to overpower Cal Tumbrel.

Tom indicated the saddle he'd used as a pillow and moved towards it. It crossed his mind that with a little improvisation the saddle could become a weapon, that he could thrust or throw it at Cal Tumbrel, catch him off guard and disarm him, but the opportunity didn't arise. The other man stepped aside so that the gun was trained on Tom's back while he carried the saddle back to the place where the sorrel was hitched.

'Hurry,' Cal ordered.

Tom worked in silence, first throwing an under-blanket across the horse to protect it from chafing, then settling the saddle in place before buckling the cinch strap under the horse's belly. He'd been hoping his opportunity would arise while he had the loose straps in his hand but his opponent, it seemed, although edgy and anxious for greater haste, had also identified this as a vulnerable moment. He stood back, out of distance from any swinging straps, but remained vigilant, watchful of every move undertaken by Tom, and his gun remained trained on Tom at all times.

The job completed, Tom untied the lead rein and fixed Cal Tumbrel with a cold stare.

'I'll catch up with you, somewhere,' he promised.

'Don't get involved,' Cal said as he climbed into the saddle.

The words puzzled Tom Belman but they quelled neither his anger nor his desire to prevent the other man from taking his horse. He didn't know the nature of the crime that had landed the youth in a prison cell nor why he had chosen to become a fugitive by breaking free, but he did know that horse-stealing wouldn't help his cause, it merely created for him another enemy. Cal must know that Tom would seek retribution if he was left in this place alive.

Cal Tumbrel turned the sorrel's head and prepared to kick his heels into its flanks. That was when he made his mistake. By turning the horse away from Tom he presented his back to the former soldier. Instantly Tom sprang forward, his left hand reaching up to grab the back of Cal's jacket and his right hand gripping the wrist of the hand that held the gun. He pulled, dragging Cal backward, his shifting weight confusing the sorrel until it was almost squatting on its hindquarters.

Unbalanced, Cal shouted with surprise but that was only momentary. In addition to trying to urge the horse forward he lashed out with the long rein in an effort to release himself from Tom's grips on his arm and clothing. The leathers snaked around Tom's shoulders and across his back but ineffectually, the blows carrying insufficient force to be anything other than a nuisance. By now the horse was upright and its nervous little jumps were making it difficult for Cal to control it while fighting off Tom's increasingly determined attack. The sorrel half-reared at the same moment as Tom put all his strength into pulling on his opponent and Cal tumbled awkwardly to the ground.

At first Tom had kept a tight grip on the hand that held the gun but as soon as his opponent fell he took the opportunity to disarm him by dashing that hand against the ground. He kicked the gun aside and stepped back. Sitting up, Cal Tumbrel muttered low curses. Tom watched him and waited for an explanation.

'I must get to the ferry,' Cal said.

'Not on my horse,' Tom told him.

Cal gathered himself into a position where he was half-sitting, half-crouching, his shoulders hunched in an attitude of defeat, but the glare in his eyes was a forewarning that he still harboured a determination to take what he wanted. Even so, when he moved it was with such suddenness that the former soldier was caught unawares. Cal barely rose above waist height but he moved with such speed that his head had butted into Tom's midriff before Tom even knew he was under attack.

Tom went over backwards, hitting the ground hard so that he was completely winded. Borne by the momentum of his charge Cal fell on top of his adversary, throwing a punch in the process that connected with the side of Tom's face. Although somewhat disoriented by this onslaught Tom's fighting spirit was not driven away. When Cal tried to struggle to his feet Tom was able to wrap his own legs around the other's ankles and send him tumbling to the ground again. Cal cursed.

'Let me go,' he demanded, an urgency in his voice that seemed, somehow, to be unrelated to the struggle that was taking place and to suggest that Tom's resistance was the wrongdoing, not his own attempted theft. But Tom grabbed Cal's jacket and pulled him closer, turned him and delivered a punch of his own that collided with Cal's jaw. Cal sprawled but kicked out at his opponent, striking Tom on the knee as he tried to approach. For several moments they struggled, wrestling on the ground, using arms, knees, feet and fists to gain the upper hand: indeed, utilizing any and every part of the body that could either inflict injury on the other or prise them free from constraining holds.

Of the two men it was clear that Tom was the stronger; his army years had created a tough and resourceful fighter. But he was still coming to terms with the headbutt in the breadbasket, finding it difficult to breathe easily, thereby making it difficult to sustain his attacks. His opponent on the other hand was fighting with unyielding resolve.

'Let me go,' Cal said more than once, still as though the fight was not about his intention to steal Tom's horse.

Each time Tom's response was to increase his efforts to overcome his opponent. Eventually it seemed that he had succeeded. They had rolled to the centre part of the clearing, close to where the fire had burned and Cal was on his back with Tom astride, ready to deliver a knockout blow to his adversary's jaw. But Cal's hand had closed around a loose rock, which he smashed against Tom's temple. It dislodged him and while he lay stunned Cal hurried across to collect the discarded pistol. He returned, gun in hand, and stood threateningly over his stunned opponent.

'This is for your own good,' he said, then he swung the iron so that it crashed against Tom's head, rendering him unconscious.

Moments later Tom struggled from the foggy depths into which he'd fallen, roused, he thought, by gunshots, but he couldn't be certain. Crazy lights were flashing inside his head and a pain throbbed with such intensity that it felt as though a gap had been opened in his skull.

Once more he descended into darkness.

2

Tom Belman poured some of his drinking water over his head, not just to wash away the blood that had run down the side of his face to the corner of his left eye, but also in the remote hope that it would reduce the intense pain he suffered with every movement. Despite this he was trying to settle on a plan of action. Although he was anxious to reclaim his horse he knew he wouldn't catch up to it on the mule, not even if he left the packs among these trees to be collected later. Indeed, he wasn't sure he would get very far at all astride the mule. Its gait induced an uncomfortable ride, every stride jostled the rider from toe to crown, and Tom needed to recover from the blow he'd taken, not suffer further aggravation. So, after recovering his weapons, he loaded the packs on the beast and, with one hand on its bridle, walked in the wake of his stolen sorrel.

Although slow, following the trail was easy. Cal Tumbrel had cut across the marks made by the galloping five but had then ridden parallel to them about two hundred yards to the south. Apart from occasional birdsong Tom's progress was marked only by the sounds produced by the movement of himself and his animal, but in his mind he remembered the gunshots that had broken through the darkness of his unconsciousness. It was a vague recollection but he was sure that the two or three shots had all been fired from the same gun. He struggled to understand them. Cal had been anxious to avoid detection when they had first seen the riders so it seemed unlikely that he had been the shooter but, if they had been fired at Cal, then why had he persisted in his dislocated pursuit.

Tom had been walking for the best part of an hour when Cal's trail took an abrupt turn to the south. There was evidence that he had quickened his pace, the hoofmarks became further apart, indicating the sorrel's long-stretched, full-gallop stride. Shortly, those marks were covered by a multitude of tracks that Tom had no hesitation in identifying as those of the group who had been on the trail ahead. Now they were in pursuit and they were all travelling fast. At this point there was a decision to make: keep going west, find the river and hope to purchase another horse at a fort or settlement along the way, or keep on the sorrel's trail and possibly walk into a heap of trouble that was none of his business. As he walked south he pondered the possibility that the crack on his head had knocked out his common sense, but the sorrel was his horse and he wanted it back.

★　★　★

The sound of a distant fusillade reached Tom before he'd covered much more than another mile. He peered ahead over the high grassland but couldn't pinpoint the location of the fight. There was no obvious motion, not even the hint of smoke rising in the air but that, he reckoned, was due to the terrain: as deceptive as a Memphis saloon woman. He walked on more cautiously, the mule plodding loyally at his side.

A whinny carried from somewhere close at hand, then a voice, shouting. Tom let the lead rope drop and walked ahead alone. All of a sudden he found himself on the lip of deep gully, a long trench that was awash with colour. The shorter grass growing there was a deeper green than the tall, tough prairie grass, but great sections of it were overpowered by clusters of white prairie fringed orchids and growing every-where were the yellow-tipped pink and orange petals of firewheels and Indian blankets. Bushes, too, were flowering or heavy with berries, and here and there tall loblolly pines reached above the top of the depression, adding to the deceptive nature of Tom's view from his position.

The colourful valley, however, held Tom's interest for barely a moment. His attention was drawn to the nearest tree, which was a stout post oak. Men were gathered around it, some mounted and others afoot. Several held rifles or pistols but the fighting seemed to be over. At the centre of the group, under a low bough of the sturdy white oak was Tom's sorrel and on its back sat Cal Tumbrel. His hands were tied behind his back and the noose at the end of a rope that had been tossed over the bough was around his neck.

Tom reacted almost at once. It might have made more sense to fire his own rifle in an effort to scatter the lynch party, but that, he figured, would make him a target for the men below. Already they had their guns in their hands and he knew they were prepared to use them. Odds of five to one weren't favourable but he couldn't stand by and watch them string up the young fellow. As he began the thirty-foot descent he yelled to the group below. All eyes turned in his direction and watched his approach.

'Mister,' said the leader of the group, the man on the chestnut mare with the deep chest, 'keep out of this. It's none of your business.'

The man spoke with the sort of assurance Tom had encountered in many of the officers he'd met in the war, men who believed in their own infallibility, that a military order was inviolable and a guarantee of success regardless of the cost or outcome. He sat like an officer, too, back straight and head high, looking straight ahead, making Tom aware that he occupied a place that was not only physically higher but in status, too. He had a big face and a full, neat moustache that probably received daily attention. But now, like the rest of the group, there was a patina of dust on his face and clothing, indicative of several hours spent in the saddle.

'Sure it is,' Tom told him. He pointed at the sorrel. 'That's my horse.'

The words sounded ridiculous. There was a guffaw and someone told him he would soon get it back.

'Who are you?' asked the man on the chestnut. 'What are you doing here?'

'My name's Tom Belman. I'm heading for California.'

Behind him someone repeated his name. 'Tom Belman.'

The voice was gruff but it carried a sarcastic tone that was not unknown to Tom. He turned to inspect the speaker and saw a face he recognized. The lanky, bare-headed man was leaning over his saddle horn, an unpleasant grin on his thin, doglike face. Like Tom, Louis Currier had been a member of Sheridan's Sixth Army Corps and for eighteen months or more they had served together, right up to Sayler's Creek, their final battle of the war. It didn't mean they were friends. Currier was a man with abilities, a good soldier apart from the fact that he always wanted more and wasn't fussy how he achieved it. There were men you could trust with your life; Currier wasn't one of them. Twice he'd been promoted as high as sergeant and twice he'd been busted back to trooper. It was rumoured he'd taken his revenge on Captain Blayney, who'd twice reduced him to the ranks, by putting a bullet in the back of his head at Sayler's Creek. The matter had never been pursued by the authorities and the death had been attributed to shrapnel from an exploding shell. Currier neither admitted nor denied the killing. The man on the chestnut spoke to Currier.

'Do you know him?'

'Sure, I know him, Mr Willis. Fought together from Gettysburg to Appamatox.'

'Do you think he's connected to this?' He threw out a hand to indicate Cal Tumbrel.

'Seems unlikely,' Currier replied, but

none the less he posed the question to Tom. 'How do you know him?'

'Met him this morning. Came upon me when I was having breakfast.'

'Where was that?' Willis asked, his words sharp as though the answer would give him some knowledge he desperately needed.

'Back east of here.'

'Where did he come from?'

Cal Tumbrel's face was pale; clearly he believed death was a certainty but his eyes were fixed on Tom as though he was willing some words into his mouth.

'The north, I guess. His horse had gone lame. He'd been forced to kill it.'

'So he stole yours!'

Tom weighed his words. Horse-stealing was a hanging offence but he had no desire to see Cal strung up. All he wanted was the return of his horse.

'He borrowed it.'

'Borrowed it? When did he mean to return it? Where was he going?'

Tom shrugged. 'I don't know. I just followed the tracks and they brought me here. I guess I'd expected him to go back north. What has he done?'

'He *borrowed* something from me, too,' said Andrew Willis, 'but I'm not as charitable as you. He won't tell me where it is so we're calling it robbery and the punishment is prescribed by law.'

Tom protested. 'Even so, you can't do it without a trial, without a representative of the law present.'

'He's had his trial and all of these men are law officers.'

Louis Currier, whose hands had been clasped on the saddle horn, pushed himself upright and swept aside the left side of his black leather waistcoat. A silver-coloured badge was attached to his dull blue shirt.

'I'm the law in Willis County, where the offence was committed,' he stated. 'Cal Tumbrel is guilty and will hang. It doesn't matter if it happens here or back in town.'

'That's not right,' Tom said.

'Sure it is, and now that we know

he's stolen a horse it makes any plea for clemency pointless. Horse thieves always hang.'

While this discussion was taking place it was clear that Andrew Willis's thoughts were fixed on another matter.

'The north,' he said. 'So they weren't heading for the ferry. I wondered why he'd drawn attention to himself. Acting as a decoy, no doubt, trying to draw us further away from the actual crossing point.' He made a noise in his throat which signified the disdain he had for Cal Tumbrel's effort at deception. He spoke to the condemned man, sneering, gloating at the perceived failure of his plan. 'Very chivalrous but a worthless sacrifice. It's a lost cause. There's only one crossing point north of the ferry and I daresay she'll be waiting there for you. I'll have her back before noon.'

Andrew Willis turned his horse away and positioned himself alongside Louis Currier, a dozen yards from the oak tree. One of the other men rode up to the condemned man and hung a roughly prepared sign around his neck. It bore the legend *Horse Thief*, which curled Currier's lips into a smirk.

'There,' he said, loosely addressing his words to Tom Belman, 'if anyone comes across his corpse they'll applaud the punishment and spit on his body.'

Tom began to protest but one of the dismounted men stepped behind the sorrel, yelled, slapped its hindquarters and chased it a few steps away from the low branch of the tree.

The five men hung around the tree long enough to watch Cal Tumbrel kick away his life, then they turned their horses to climb out the gully. The quickest route to the northern crossing point was across country, and Mr Willis was in a hurry. Louis Currier had words for Tom Belman before riding away.

'Usually, a stolen horse becomes the property of the court until we get adequate proof of ownership. But in your case we'll make an exception. After all, you've been useful to us, proved beyond all doubt that the kid deserved to hang.' He grinned at the simmering anger that showed on Tom's face. 'But I suggest you put a good few miles between you and this place. The matter's finished. Keep heading west, soldier.'

When he'd gone Tom brought his mule down from the lip of the gully, took a shovel from his pack and dug a grave for Cal Tumbrel. It seemed the least he could do for the young man. Even though the possibility of anyone finding the body in this isolated part of the country was remote it rankled that the dead man's ignominious death might be taken as a testament to his life. Tom acknowledged that he'd hardly known Cal Tumbrel long enough to have any opinion of his character, and it was true that the young man had taken his horse despite Tom's best effort to prevent it, but he couldn't escape the feeling that Cal's need and determination had been born of something greater than personal gain. The comments made by Andrew Willis had added credence to that belief. Tom was gripped by an awful sense of guilt, that his intervention had hastened Cal's death. His reckless statements had labelled Cal a horse thief and that epithet had legitimized the lynching.

While he worked he considered the events of the morning, remembered particularly Cal's insistence that he needed to get to the ferry. The ferry, Tom gathered, had been the destination of the other horsemen too, until Cal had lured them away from that trail. Willis had been right to suspect that Cal was acting as a decoy, but only to get him away from the ferry. The assumption that the woman he was seeking was on a trail further north was wrong.

Tom gained a small amount of solace from the fact that he had, unwittingly, sent the group in the wrong direction. He recalled the expression on Cal's face when it became clear that the pursuit had been sent off course. His eyes had sought out Tom, transmitting a message, it seemed, that they had only achieved a delay: the job was only half done.

Tom threw the last shovelful of soil on to the grave, then repacked the load on the mule. He had a need for being submerged in water but when he rode away from the gully the urgent need he felt to reach the river had nothing to do with cleanliness.

3

Andrew Willis, upright in the saddle, led the way north, retracing the tracks that Cal Tumbrel had made after taking Tom Belman's sorrel. When they reached the forsaken campsite they halted, horses blowing from the exertion. A lot had been asked of them since leaving Ortega Point.

'The horses need a rest,' Louis Currier announced.

'The horses are fine,' snapped Willis, 'there's plenty of running in them.'

'Yeah,' Currier agreed, 'if they're allowed to run at their own speed. Not at the pace you're setting.'

'They'll have to keep up. We've got a lot of ground to cover.'

Louis Currier smirked. 'If they could keep up then you'd have wasted your money. I reckon you could have bought a string of these critturs for the price of that chestnut.'

His words brought grins to the faces of the other three riders; their boss was a man who enjoyed his superiority, who wanted everything he had to be better than everyone else's. Andrew Willis wasn't amused. He didn't like the men he employed talking to him as if they knew more than he did but he needed to walk softly around Louis Currier. The sheriff was a violent man, ever eager to show his ability with the pistol that hung in a holster on his right thigh. Willis wasn't eager to cross him, unless it was to double-cross him. One day, he thought, it would come to that: he'd shoot him when he didn't expect it, when he was unarmed or presented his back as a target. For now, though, he voiced his anger at the other three. They had neither the courage to fight him nor the ability to win if they did. Besides, they liked the money he paid so he could abuse them as often as he chose and they wouldn't rebel.

Currier ran his sleeved forearm

across his brow.

'Perhaps we're doing the wrong thing, heading north,' he said.

'What do you mean?'

'I'm asking myself why the kid needed to attract our attention.'

'To drag us away from the girl,' Willis explained, his tone implying that such an explanation should have been unnecessary.

'Yeah,' said Currier, 'but if they were using the north crossing we were already on the wrong trail. If he'd remained undetected and ridden north we wouldn't have caught them before crossing the river.'

'You think she might be waiting for him at the ferry?'

'It's possible. We need to know for sure. If you send someone to check they can rejoin us upriver if she's not there.'

Andrew Willis let the possibility float in his mind for a moment, not because there was fault in the logic of Currier's suggestion but because a hasty agreement might encourage the man to think his views were important. Eventually he looked at the threesome who wore deputy badges pinned to their shirts.

'Charlie Fairfax,' he said, 'you ride down to the ferry. If you find her, hold her there until we arrive.'

Charlie threw a glance towards Currier, hoping he would press the point about the horses needing rest, but the sheriff showed no further interest in the subject so Charlie turned his animal and set off in the direction of the Canadian. He had it in his head to stop awhile as soon as he was out of sight of the others. Only a foolish man would run his horse to death and leave himself afoot miles away from home.

Curtis Kennedy, another of the deputies, had dismounted to inspect the campsite. From its high point he could see the snaking line of trodden grass coming up the hill from the north. He pointed it out to the others, emphasizing that it had not been created by a horse.

'Follow that and we should come

across his dead animal. When we find it we'll know we're on the right trail.'

'Let's go then,' commanded Andrew Willis, and he kicked his horse on its way down the hill before Curtis had time to remount.

A gap developed between Willis and the other three riders. Willis maintained it to emphasize his aloofness and the others didn't try to close it because it would have been foolhardy to do so.

They'd travelled eight miles before finding the carcass. The dead horse was still saddled. It had a broken leg and a severed neck artery. Cal Tumbrel had used a knife on the animal rather than risk alerting anyone in the vicinity of their location by putting a bullet in its brain.

'In the dark it must have taken him more than an hour to reach that campsite.'

The same thought flitted through the minds of all the men. Had Cal Tumbrel gone in that direction deliberately to steal a horse? Had he seen a glimmer of flame on the far-off knoll? They would never know. What they did know was that a second horse, the girl's, had cut a trail at right angles to the one trodden by Cal Tumbrel.

'Not heading for the north crossing,' Curtis Kennedy offered when he ranged alongside Andrew Willis. 'Once around that hillside it's a straight run to the river.'

'I reckon she's far enough ahead to be across the river,' Louis Currier stated. He cast a look at Willis, wondering what he would do now. In his opinion they should get back to Ortega Point, pack up the equipment and flee to some place where they could start again.

'She hasn't crossed the river,' Willis declared. 'Why would he try to decoy us south if she was already safe? No, she's waiting for him. She'll be at the ferry. We'll catch her there.'

They dismounted, rested the horses for an hour, confident that either she would soon be the prisoner of Charlie

Fairfax, or he would chase her into their clutches as they followed the river south to Domingo's Ferry.

★   ★   ★

Less than fifty years earlier, seeking fresh grazing, a man called Ortega had brought his sheep and his family up into this remote part of the Texas panhandle from the Red River country. He prospered from the move. His reputation for hospitality coincided with increased traffic along the Santa Fe trail and soon it became necessary to extend the home he'd built near an old trading fort to provide eating quarters and sleeping berths for weary travellers. From that small beginning had grown the town of Ortega Point which, after the discovery of gold in California in 1849, became the site of an army outpost established to protect the thousands of prospectors heading west. Ortega, a sheepman at heart, returned south with his flocks but the town bearing his name continued to flourish.

At that time Pablo Domingo had been married to one of Ortega's sisters. They had built their home on the banks of the Canadian River, and just as the traffic along the Santa Fe trail had increased so had the number of people seeking a route across the Canadian River. Pablo soon realized that something more substantial than a rowing boat was needed to transport people with animals and carts from one bank to the other. He constructed a huge, flat craft with a rope-and-winch system which, harnessed to oxen, enabled him to haul people and goods safely across the river. Now his son, Enrique, in addition to tending a small flock of sheep, had replaced him as the ferryman.

Fever had taken Enrique's wife some years earlier so his only permanent help was his twelve-year-old son, Felipe. It was Felipe who first saw the young woman that morning as she coaxed a weary horse along the riverside trail, peering ahead suspiciously and occasionally turning to anxiously scan the eastern approaches.

Fifty yards from the buildings the girl dismounted, as though fearful that her animal would collapse if she remained in the saddle. As she walked she wrapped an arm around the horse's head, although whether that was to give solace to the animal or support for herself was difficult to discern. Perhaps it was both. When she saw the young lad watching her from the stoop of his house she paused and seemed reassured by the tranquil demeanour he presented. Bare-headed, his dull-red poncho lightly disturbed by the valley breeze, he put down the buckets he'd been carrying to the house, his morning routine interrupted by her arrival. It had been almost twenty-four hours since she'd last slept but now relief conquered her tiredness. A smile almost showed on her dust-covered face. No one had beaten her to the river crossing.

She clapped her filly's neck, let it know she was pleased with it. For a while, until Cal joined them, it could rest, then they would cross the river and head home. The horse trembled; it had given everything to carry her here but now it was exhausted and Cal had been right to refuse to ride double when his own horse fell. Although the filly was game, her abilities were limited and she would have collapsed before reaching the river. Her memory of chasing the string of horses on to the prairie when they made their escape from Ortega Point niggled. If they'd held on to a couple, used them when their own had tired, they would be safely beyond the reach of Sheriff Currier's men. But, she corrected herself, such an act would have given the Ortega Point men a valid reason to arrest them. It would have been horse-stealing and there was only one sentence for anyone guilty of that crime.

Cal had convinced her that the distant light he'd seen came from a campfire and that he would be able to persuade someone to sell him a mount. She didn't know why she'd let him go. He was taking a risk on her behalf that she hadn't earned. He'd already risked his own safety to rescue her, bursting into the room where she was held captive and holding the deputies at gun-point. She didn't know how he'd found her, hadn't even known that he was searching for her; she thought he'd returned to Amarillo, but he'd planned the escape, had even untied the other horses from the rail before rescuing her so they'd been able to drive them ahead when they raced out of town.

All would have been well if his horse hadn't fallen. If he failed to find another one he faced a long walk and the risk of being overtaken if Andrew Willis had sent men in pursuit. Once again, her eyes turned to the east. How glad she would be when he appeared on that ridge. His last instruction had been to cross the river and keep riding until she reached her father in Amarillo. It was an instruction she wouldn't obey. He had risked danger to save her, she wouldn't cross the river without him.

Felipe tended to the filly while his father fussed around the young woman. Sally Locke was a regular visitor, always stopping for coffee when she made the journey to Ortega Point with copies of the *Amarillo Gazette*, a weekly publication from her father's press. This day, Enrique Domingo was troubled by the anxiety showing on Sally's face. His concern, however, was unassuaged, Sally evaded his questions with the skill of a politician. She had determined to keep secret the events that had taken place in Ortega Point: the less Enrique Domingo knew the less he could reveal if Sheriff Currier arrived to question him. She told him she needed him to ferry her across the river when Cal Tumbrel arrived.

Although exhausted, she couldn't rest. She climbed the small hill behind the house, from where she had a good view across the prairie land. With her back pressed against the trunk of a wide-spreading cottonwood, she focused on the land beyond the eastern ridge. She had been watching for an hour when the first movement, the first hint of a break on the skyline, caught her attention. As the vague shape developed into a distinctive form she could tell that there was only one rider. The tension contained within her was released with a sob of joy. Cal had succeeded in his quest. In the past twenty-four hours he had proved himself more resourceful than she had ever deemed likely. Yet here he was, a horse under him, coming fast to join her. They would soon be across the Canadian and on the road to Amarillo.

For several minutes she continued to watch; she considered waving but her limbs suddenly felt too heavy to respond to her thoughts, as though the release of tension had simultaneously taken the strength from her muscles. She felt pleasantly giddy for a brief moment, then she fixed her gaze on the approaching rider with more critical intent.

It took less than a moment for Sally Locke to realize what it was that now roused in her some uncertainty. It was the rider's hat: not a high-domed Texas hat of the kind favoured by Cal, but a flat-crowned Stetson. Also the shape of the rider was wrong: it was more squat, bulkier than the long slim body of her youthful friend. As she turned, using the trunk of the tree to hide from the newcomer, a sob of despair escaped from her mouth. The sudden plunge from elation to despair had taken her by surprise. She began to run, hampered by fatigue but spurred on by the realization that she knew the rider. It was Charlie Fairfax, one of the deputies who had kept her captive.

Enrique Domingo saw the girl stumble and roll down the hill in an ungainly rush to reach his house. Panic showed in her wide-open brown eyes but she was sure she could trust the ferryman to assist her.

'There's a man coming,' she blurted, 'a deputy from Ortega Point. He mustn't find me.'

In addition to their living quarters, Domingo's estate consisted of a number of smaller buildings. The largest of those was the stable for the animals. Felipe was near the doorway, preparing to take the oxen down to the river to drink.

Enrique pointed to the building.

'Quickly,' he said, 'cover yourself with Felipe's poncho.' Then, pointing at the stable, he added, 'you'll find an old straw sombrero in there that will hide your face. Stay there. If he sees you he'll think you're my son. I'll tell him I haven't seen you.'

The smell in the stable was unpleasant and as she rammed the old sombrero on to her head Sally wished she'd replaced Felipe completely and taken the animals down the river. But another, more troubling thought occurred to her. She didn't want Enrique to say that he hadn't seen her; it would be better if he told Charlie Fairfax that he'd taken her across the river. She would be safer if the men from Ortega Point believed she was out of their reach.

She stepped outside and looked across the yard, wondering if she had time to reach the house, get that message to Señor Domingo, but already the sound of the horse's steps was loud across the ground. Man and rider swung into view and Sally Locke hurried back into the stable's stench.

Charlie Fairfax assumed that the figure he saw disappearing into the barn was the ferryman's son. The lad was always around to help his father when there was a need to carry traffic across the river. He dismounted, stepped up on to the stoop and went inside the building where passengers were allowed to wait.

Charlie didn't waste time on formalities, merely pulled aside the left side of his waistcoat to show the badge pinned on to his shirt.

'Do you know Sally Locke?' he asked Enrique. 'Her father prints the *Amarillo Gazette*.'

'*Sí*, I know her.'

'Is she here?'

'No, *señor*. There's no one here but my son and me.'

'When did you last see her?'

Enrique shrugged, then pointed to the far bank of the Canadian.

'I brought her across two, perhaps three days ago.'

'You haven't seen her since?'

'No, *señor*.'

The information wasn't unexpected; in Charlie's opinion it had always been more likely that the woman would use the north crossing. He knew he should mount up and hurry along the river trail to meet up with Lou Currier and the others but the smell of strong coffee filled the room and he decided he could spare a few minutes to refresh himself if the ferryman could spare him a cup.

He'd already taken time out to rest his horse but it would welcome a few more minutes without him in the saddle.

Five minutes later he gathered up the reins, and climbed on to the back of the animal but before heading north he rode down to the water's edge and allowed it to drink from the swift-flowing river. Charlie's attention was caught by a movement downstream. A boy was hard at work washing a pale ox while another animal, darker in colour, waited patiently in the shade of a low willow. At the moment when Charlie recognized the ferryman's son he also recalled the figure he'd seen hurrying into the barn on his arrival. Were they the same person? He couldn't see any sign of a poncho or sombrero along the riverbank where the bare-chested boy was at work. He twisted in the saddle and looked back towards the buildings. The ferryman was watching him, rubbing his hands on a piece of cloth as though drying them. The nervous gesture didn't escape the notice of

Charlie Fairfax. He turned his horse and rode directly to the barn.

★ ★ ★

Since acquiring the mule back in Topeka there had been few occasions when Tom Belman had demanded anything faster from it than a steady trot, a pace that had never been sustained for more than a couple of miles. This morning was different; the long run across the grasslands was prompted by a compulsion to reach the ferry crossing on the Canadian River as quickly as possible. Common sense told him that he hadn't been responsible for the death of the youth but, since he had been unable to prevent it, he was gripped by a sense of obligation to undertake the task that had been left unfulfilled. Cal had been prepared to die to keep a woman safe from Willis; now it was up to him to do what he could for her protection. The first step was to find her and warn her of the imminent danger.

Tom didn't know the location of the northern river crossing, nor how far the posse would ride before discovering they were on a wild-goose chase. When they did they would race back to the ferry. It was essential to get the woman away from there before they turned up. The message of urgency travelled to his heels and from thence to the sorrel's flanks. Horse and mule responded without complaint.

He had seen the dust of a rider ahead of him for a mile before reaching the ridge that overlooked the crossing point on the Canadian. Halting on the crest he recognized the rider as one of the deputies who had been present at the lynching of Cal Tumbrel. Someone in the group hadn't dismissed the possibility of the woman heading for the ferry. That, Tom figured, would be Mr Willis, or perhaps Currier who had always had a shrewd battle sense.

The trail down from the ridge took the rider behind the little group of buildings that comprised Enrique Domingo's estate, making him blind to the activity that was being conducted between the main house and the barn. From his position on the ridge, however, Tom saw the tumbling run of the woman down the opposite hillside, saw her don the boy's poncho and make her way to the far barn.

When Tom descended he didn't follow the trail to the front of the buildings. Instead he dismounted and walked his animals to the rear of the barn in which the woman had taken refuge. He had hoped to find another door into the building but there was none. He edged swiftly but cautiously along the side of the building and paused at the end. He could see the deputy's horse hitched outside the largest building and guessed that he was inside talking with the ferryman. He pulled open the door and led the horse and mule into the darkness.

An intake of air, almost silent, testified to the fact that the woman had been startled by the abrupt opening of the barn door. She was standing towards the rear of the barn, almost invisible in the darkness except for the whiteness of her eyes which were turned in Tom's direction.

'Are you the one Willis is after?' Tom asked. He could hear her breathing but she didn't reply.

'Is the ferryman helping you? What is he telling him?'

'That he hasn't seen me. Who are you?'

For the moment, Tom ignored her question.

'The deputy might go without taking a look around,' he told her, 'but you need to hide in case he comes in here. Give me that poncho,' he ordered. 'I think he saw you wearing it. Hide in one of the stalls until he's gone.'

'Who are you?' she asked again, her voice quiet and apprehensive.

'I'm the man whose horse Cal stole.'

'Cal! Is he with you?'

Hoofbeats of a cantering horse

sounded from the other side of the door. Tom pulled the poncho over his head and set the too-small sombrero on his head. The young woman bent low behind the wooden planks of a stall just as sunlight spread into the fetid barn.

Tom, crouching slightly to disguise his true height, kept his back to the light, allowing the deputy to approach. Charlie Fairfax held his pistol in his right hand, put his left on Tom's shoulder and spun him around. Whatever words he'd meant to utter remained in his mouth when he recognized the man facing him.

'You,' Charlie eventually said. 'What are you doing here?' He turned to look at Enrique Domingo who had followed him to the barn and now stood in the doorway. 'You said there was no one here but you and your boy.'

Enrique spread his arms, shrugged, as though his forgetfulness could be attributed to his nationality. Didn't Americans think that all Mexicans were fat, lazy and stupid?

'I got here just ahead of you,' lied Tom. 'Perhaps he thought we were together.'

Eyeing with suspicion Tom's poncho and sombrero, Charlie Fairfax wanted to know his reason for wearing them.

'Protection from all the dust I'm likely to brush out of these animals.' Tom indicated the horse and mule that hadn't yet been unharnessed.

For Charlie it was an unconvincing explanation. There were plenty of travelling hours left in the day, so why wasn't this pilgrim making the most of them? The only reason for coming to this ferry point was to cross the river. Domingo might provide a meal or even a bed in emergencies, but it wasn't his usual practice. Why was this Yankee soldier preparing to groom his animals, and why do it in this stinking barn? Outside the air was fresh and there was a river to wash them in just a handful of yards away.

He regarded the packs that were strapped on either side of the mule and wondered what they held. Was there something of value in them? Was the ex-soldier's strange behaviour an artifice to deflect attention away from the goods he was carrying?

He motioned with the gun that was still held in his right hand, ordering Tom to step aside.

Tom ignored him, reluctant to let the deputy get nearer the animals. The girl was in the stall just behind them and likely to be discovered if Charlie Fairfax got too close.

'Stand clear,' Charlie told Tom. Tom wanted to know why. 'I want to check your load.'

'You've got no reason to do that.'

'Sure I do.' Charlie used the barrel of his gun to tap the badge on his chest. 'This gives me all the reason I need. After all, this is the third time you've got in the way, tried to hamper the process of law.'

'Third time?' exclaimed Tom; his thoughts were back in the prairie gully where what he'd witnessed was difficult to associate with a process of the law.

'Yesterday you refused to allow your horse to be used in pursuit of escaping prisoners and this morning you tried to interfere when sentence was being carried out on a man guilty of horse-stealing. It was your horse that he'd stolen.'

Tom's jaw tightened. He hoped the young woman hadn't connected the deputy's reference to horse-stealing with Cal Tumbrel. It was a vain hope. A sound carried, reached everyone's ears: a clatter as something wooden was struck and rolled on the ground.

The words she'd heard the deputy utter had shocked Sally Locke. Clearly, someone had been hanged for horse-stealing and Cal had left her in search of a mount to get him to Amarillo. Although she fought against it, she felt compelled to step forward and confront the lawman. Crouched against the wooden spars she thrust back her left leg. In the interior gloom she hadn't noticed the wooden water bucket but now it tipped and rolled a little way, betraying her presence to everyone in the barn.

'Cal,' she said, her head showing above the stall rails, 'what have you done to him?'

But Charlie Fairfax wasn't interested in her question. Although surprised by her sudden appearance the only thought it provoked was that he was the one who had caught her. Mr Willis would be pleased.

'There you are,' he said. 'You're going back to Ortega Point. There'll be no escape this time.'

'She's not going anywhere with you,' Tom Belman stated.

Charlie Fairfax motioned with his gun, a declaration that he was holding all the power.

'This and the badge say she is. She's got to face the law.'

'I've seen your interpretation of the law. Whatever she's done it's clear she won't get justice in Ortega Point. She's not going back there with you.'

'I don't think you can prevent it,' Charlie Fairfax told him.

He swung the gun around to point it at Tom but the ex-soldier was already moving. His left hand had formed into a fist and it travelled in a short arc, hooking into Charlie's gut just above the belt. The Ortega Point lawman doubled over, the gun in his hand forgotten as he tried to suck air into his body. Tom swept the gun arm aside and the pistol fell to the ground. Then he stepped close to his opponent and swung a punch at his jaw. Charlie Fairfax staggered backwards, towards the open door. Another combination, a left to the body followed by a right cross to the jaw, sent him sprawling in the outside dust.

'Come on,' Tom told the young woman. 'We've got to get clear of this place.' He grabbed the lead reins of his animals to take them outside but the woman's horse had been unsaddled and several minutes had to be spent making it ready for the trail. Enrique

Domingo wanted to ferry them across the river but Tom waved away the offer.

'That would be too dangerous for you,' Tom told him, thinking about the punishment meted out to Cal Tumbrel. 'If that deputy tells Willis that you helped us he'll probably kill you. We'll find another route across the river.' He looked at Sally Locke. 'I hope the law in Amarillo is more just than it is at this side of the river.'

'I haven't done anything,' she told him.

He wanted to believe her but there was no time for any discussion.

When they went back outside Charlie Fairfax had moved from the place where he'd lain senseless. His pistol was still inside the barn and his horse was still hitched to the rail outside the far building. Tom spotted the empty rifle scabbard under the deputy's saddle and knew Charlie Fairfax was waiting to ambush him when he left the barn. For the first time since the end of the war Tom knew the tingle of apprehension that he'd always experienced when danger threatened.

Using the open door as a shield he scanned the surrounding area. He studied the corners of every building but caught no movement. Somewhere, however, the deputy was waiting for him and was aware that there was only one way out of the barn.

Tom had to make Charlie reveal his position. To do that meant presenting himself as a target. He told Enrique and the young woman to remain inside the barn; then, stooping, he raced outside and threw himself forward. A flatboard wagon with a broken wheel stood opposite the barn door and Tom had assessed the advantages of using it as a cover from which he could defend himself against the deputy's fire. It would also give him scope to launch an attack of his own. Charlie Fairfax, he'd decided, had to be using one of the buildings between the barn and the horse as his ambush point. He was wrong.

As Tom had done earlier, Charlie had made his way around the rear of all the buildings until he reached the far side of the barn. His plan was to be behind Tom when he left the barn and if Tom's outrush hadn't been executed with such surprising speed he would surely have been shot before he was clear of the doorway. However, Charlie had barely gained the optimum spot from which to fire before Tom dashed out and tumbled and rolled across the space towards the ill-balanced vehicle.

Charlie fired; his bullets smacked the ground all around Tom's body. Tom, surprised at first by the position of his enemy, fired as he rolled. When the war ended he had thought he would never shoot at another man again, but when someone was trying to kill you it displaced every moral argument.

Charlie had stepped away from the side of the building, made himself an open target. He staggered back when the first bullet hit him in the chest, his knees buckled when the second hit him

in the gut and he crashed to the ground
dead when the third put a hole in his
forehead.

4

Tom Belman, Sally Locke and Enrique Domingo gathered around the body that was bleeding out on to the hard-packed ground in front of the barn.

'What do we do with him?' asked Sally.

The same question had occurred to Tom and it needed an answer that absolved Enrique and his son from any involvement in the deputy's death. Willis and his men could turn up at any moment and would demand answers from the ferryman if the body remained in sight. Tom looked across the river, wondering if Willis and his men could be convinced that their comrade had gone in pursuit of Sally, but she was quick to reject that idea. The Canadian was the boundary line between counties; Sheriff Currier and his deputies

70

had no authority on the other side of the river.

The alternative seemed to be for Enrique to deny that Charlie Fairfax had ever reached the landing stage, but that could be easily disproved. The high bank above the river, stretching back a mile, was made of hard rock in which it was difficult to identify marks made by an individual horse, but beyond the bank, in the softer terrain of the grassland, the fresh tracks could easily be traced back to the abandoned campsite where he'd parted company from the rest of the posse.

'We'll have to leave him up among those rocks, make it seem as though he never reached here. Señor Domingo,' Tom said, 'can you cover up the blood? When he gets here, tell Willis that you haven't seen the deputy.'

'And the *señorita*?'

'Tell him you took her across the river early this morning.' He looked at Sally for approval. Nothing in the expression on her face implied that she was bestowing it but at least she didn't argue. 'How far is it to Amarillo?' he asked.

'Twenty miles,' she told him.

'Then pursuit would be pointless. They wouldn't expect to catch you before you reached the town and once there they won't have a warrant to take you back to Ortega Point.'

'Nor a reason,' she told him, a barbed retort, disclaiming any wrongdoing on her part.

Tom let the comment pass; he wasn't interested in the cause of the dispute that had put her in the Ortega Point jail but he was sure that it hadn't been severe enough to warrant the death of her young friend. They would take the body up into the high ground and remain there until Willis and his men had returned to their own town. Then they would cross the river; she would return home and he would continue his journey west to the far sierras.

With the body of Charlie Fairfax thrown across the saddle Tom Belman trailed the horse back up the road to the hard high ground. Sally Locke rode at his side and remained silent until they were picking a path among the crags and boulders from which they could watch the events at the ferry point unobserved.

'How did Cal die?' she suddenly asked.

Tom studied her face, noted the firm line of her mouth, the determined look in the large brown eyes that held his own in an unblinking gaze. He knew there was nothing to be gained by trying to soften the manner of his death; shame or glory, silently or screaming, dead was dead and there was no coming back.

'They hanged him.'

Silence settled between them for a few more seconds. Tom knew he'd merely confirmed the woman's thoughts. She spoke again.

'Because he stole your horse?'

He told her the full story from Cal reaching his camp up to the violent ending in the gully.

'They used my horse as justification for what they did, but they already had the noose around Cal's neck. Willis said he'd stolen something from him. I took him to mean you.'

'I don't belong to Andrew Willis!' she snapped.

'Perhaps not, but he was the reason you were being held in jail.'

'I wasn't in jail,' she said, her eyes flashing at him with anger.

'I was in Ortega Point yesterday morning when you made the breakout, standing on the street when the stampeded horses went by.'

'I wasn't in jail,' she repeated. 'I haven't committed any crime. They caught me in Willis's office and were holding me there until they could get him in from his farmhouse.'

Tom Belman told her he'd always believed that breaking into someone else's property was a crime. He could see an argument brewing, her head lifted in an antagonistic attitude and there was fire in her eyes, but reason got the better of her and her voice was more conciliatory when she eventually spoke.

'Not as great a crime as his.'

At first Tom assumed she was referring to the killing of Cal Tumbrel, but then he realized that she was referring to her reason for being in Willis's office.

'What were you doing in his office?' he asked.

Her reply wasn't instantly forthcoming, her reticence in acquainting him with her business was born of a natural reluctance to share details about herself with a stranger together with the professional creed of a newspaper writer to guard her story. But this man had already killed to protect her and, according to his story, had tried to save Cal from the rope, acts which had earned him a bit of trust.

'I was looking for evidence,' she told him.

Tom remained silent, waiting for

more details; Sally knew that that titbit alone wouldn't satisfy him.

'I think he's responsible for the counterfeit money that is flooding the state.'

Tom had been hearing talk about false notes for several weeks. Barmen in Arkansas had viewed new bills of all denominations with suspicion but, to the best of his knowledge, Tom had had none in his possession. During the war, he'd known a man in his platoon who claimed he'd been involved in forging Confederate dollars that had been spread throughout the Southern states as part of a plot to weaken their finances. He was never sure if Gary Hudson's story was true, or, more specifically, whether he'd actually been involved in such a scheme; soldiers told tales as tall as those of the old mountain men, but later, at the end of the conflict, there was plenty of confirmation of such Union activities.

'My father runs a newspaper in Amarillo,' Sally began, 'the *Amarillo*

Gazette,' she added with not a little pride. 'A week ago we received a shipment of paper and inks. When they were being unloaded we saw an ink consignment that was destined for Ortega Point. That town has never had its own newspaper, in fact we've always handled all their printing needs. On closer scrutiny we knew that the inks were of a colour and kind more specialized than those commonly used for newspaper print. They were oil-based inks, the kind that wouldn't smudge when rubbed, green and red in addition to black.

'We were curious about the kind of competition we were facing, so I decided that when I next visited Ortega Point I would do a bit of snooping. My father was against it, of course, telling me not to get into any trouble. Well, that wasn't my intention, I just wanted to know what areas of our business would be affected by the new printer. Cal, of course, didn't want me to go alone but Dad wouldn't let him accompany me because he was needed around the office.

'So, as usual when the latest edition of the Gazette was printed, I made the trip to Ortega Point. At first my enquiries about a new printer got me nowhere. No one was aware of a new business in Ortega Point. Then I saw Cal. He'd disobeyed my father and followed me. I was annoyed with him. Dad needed him, I didn't.'

She paused, thought about what she'd said, then took a deep breath. She looked up at Tom from under lowered lids, knowing that what she'd said sounded churlish. She knew the lad had lost his life because of her; she hadn't meant to belittle him, just couldn't explain his behaviour or, probably, her own.

'Guess he liked me,' she conceded; then with sadness, 'I know he liked me.' Thinking about the lad changed her face, the muscles losing the tightness of tension so that her cheeks lost their hollowed appearance and her jaw its sharp, bony squareness. Her lips, too, appeared softer and fuller, banishing the grimness that had been depicted by their former tight-pressed line. She continued her story:

'I told Cal that I'd taken a room in town and that he had to return to Amarillo, but before he left we ate at Mrs Pinder's eating house. One of the sheriff's deputies, Jim Bolton, was at one of the tables with another man whom I didn't know. I didn't really take much notice of them until they were leaving, then I noticed the green stains on the stranger's finger. Our printer gets similar black stains on his hands when he's working the press. Mrs Pinder didn't know the man's name but she was sure he was employed by Andrew Willis.'

'So you thought you'd found your printer,' said Tom. 'What made you think he was printing counterfeit money?'

Sally looked a bit abashed. 'Hunch,' she said, 'coincidence, intuition. Any of those, nothing more at first. Mrs Pinder examining the notes I paid her with. Associating the type of ink and colour with the greenbacks in her hand. You'll think me silly, but that was the starting point.'

'That was reason enough for you to break into Andrew Willis's office?' Tom asked.

'Of course not,' she said. 'Cal argued against me remaining in Ortega Point but I insisted and told him to go home. After he'd gone I asked around about Andrew Willis, where he'd come from and how he'd made his money. Nobody could provide definite answers. He turned up after the war and bought the farm east of town. There's usually half a dozen men out there but there doesn't seem to be enough livestock to warrant so many hands. But Willis always has money and has gained a lot of influence hereabouts. The new sheriff, a man called Lou Currier, is in his pocket. Some people think that Willis brought Currier to Ortega Point.'

'Who did you speak to?'

'People who've lived in Ortega Point a while, Dr Carter, Mrs Walcroft who runs the boarding house, Mr Finister and his wife at the emporium. One or two others. Told them I was gathering information about the town because my dad was thinking about producing a local newspaper for Ortega Point.'

Tom said, 'You spoke to Sam Dack. You convinced him that he was going to be chief reporter for the new paper.'

'You know Mr Dack?' The question was edged with embarrassment.

'Chirpy as a cricket because he thinks he'll be an important man in the town.'

'I know some people think he's an old windbag but it's not so. As a young man he was a member of John Fremont's third expedition, which reached California, and he was a soldier in Colonel Kearny's Army of the West in the war with Mexico. He talks to everyone, he's a natural information gatherer.' She paused, still abashed by the thought that Tom Belman considered her manipulative.

'He'll get paid for anything he passes on that can be used in the *Gazette*,' she told him, then, tilting her head and looking unflinchingly into Tom's eyes, she added, 'Every good journalist needs a dependable source for their information.'

On another occasion Tom Belman might have been amused by Sally's attempt to define her behaviour as 'professional etiquette'.

'Sam Dack doesn't need me to argue on his behalf,' was all he said. 'I'm sure he's as capable of taking care of himself as you are.'

For a moment Sally thought Tom's remark was some kind of criticism with regard to her behaviour towards Cal Tumbrel, but he'd pulled his horse to a halt and was beginning to dismount. She watched while he pulled the body off the horse and draped it over a low boulder so that it would be more easily seen when the rest of the posse came looking for him.

'Go on with your story,' Tom told the young woman. 'I'm still not sure why you think Willis is the counterfeiter.'

Sally removed her hat and her fair hair tumbled down on to her shoulders. She saw Tom Belman's head turn in her direction and noted the appreciative look in his eyes. She undid the yellow bandanna that was tied around her neck and used it to wipe around the inside of her hat before tucking the hair back inside and replacing it on her head.

'I guess the most important thing I learned about Andrew Willis is that no one knows how he earned his money. He certainly has plenty and is usually generous in support of any of the town's enterprises. The more I talked to people the more suspicious I became. Then, late in the afternoon, Jim Bolton, the deputy I'd seen in Mrs Pinder's eating place, stopped me on the street, gripped my arms and drew me into an alley. He'd heard I'd been asking questions about Andrew Willis and warned me against it. I said I was gathering information for an article the *Gazette* was preparing about important people in the area but he told me to forget it. His manner was threatening and he told me to get out of town.'

'He frightened you?'

'A bit,' she admitted, 'but I wasn't going to be scared away. I went back to my room to plan my next step. Rather than make me quit the investigation, the deputy's rough manner made me more convinced that Andrew Willis had something to hide. I knew that neither he nor Sheriff Currier were in town, so I waited until dark, until the town was asleep, then I made my way to Willis's office.'

'What did you expect to find?'

Sally shrugged. 'I don't know. I guess I was just hoping there would be something that would point to him being the forger.'

'Was there?'

'I don't know; I was caught almost

before I got inside the building. I was tied to a chair and Deputies Bolton and Fairfax remained with me while a third man went out to the farm to bring back Willis and the sheriff.'

'So you don't have any positive proof against him?'

'They wouldn't kill Cal for rescuing me if they didn't have something to hide.'

Tom was forced to confess that that argument alone gave credence to her suspicion. They'd hanged Cal Tumbrel but it was the young woman they were most anxious to catch. Tom could only assume it was because of her association with the *Amarillo Gazette*. Andrew Willis, he supposed, was unwilling to have details about himself circulated across the state.

Sally Locke had her back to the river, looking across the grasslands towards Ortega Point.

'I won't let them get away with killing Cal,' she said. 'Back there I'll find some evidence of Willis's involvement with counterfeit money.'

'Don't be a fool,' Tom told her. 'If they catch you again they won't show any mercy. They'll kill you just as surely as they killed Cal.'

She sat silently astride the horse, turned her head to look at Tom; the lines of her face hardened again, an argument was brewing in her brain. Her gaze wandered to the slumped body of Charlie Fairfax as though weighing his death against Cal's and finding the scales still unbalanced.

Tom, too, looked in the direction of the corpse; that was when he noticed the empty gun holster on the dead deputy's hip. He recalled the pistol lying on the floor of the barn where it had been dropped during the fight. If, by chance, it was found by one of the posse when they reached the ferry they would know that Enrique Domingo's denial that Charlie Fairfax had ever been there was a lie. He looked back towards the river but there was no sign of activity; Willis and his men were still somewhere upstream.

Tom told Sally that he had to go and retrieve the gun.

'Wait here,' he told her. 'Find a place where we can watch without being seen. When I return we'll wait until the posse rides back to Ortega Point, then we'll cross the river together. You'll be safe in Amarillo. Tell the law about your suspicions and Cal's death. Let them pursue the matter.'

He put his spurs to the horse's flanks and raced back down to Domingo's ferry.

★　★　★

Ever since the early arrival of Señorita Locke the day had been heavy with expectation for Felipe Domingo. The young woman's grubby and exhausted appearance had clearly startled his normally placid father. Perhaps Enrique's discomposure was the cause of the dreadful expectation that filled the boy's mind, an inexplicable sense of foreboding. Later, when the sound of gunfire had reached him at the riverside, Felipe had abandoned the oxen and, fearing for his father's safety, rushed up to the buildings of his home. He'd witnessed his father and another man hoisting the deputy's body across a horse which the stranger had then led away, back up the escarpment to the prairie land beyond. The señorita had gone with them and his father had set to work clearing away the dead man's blood.

When Enrique had seen his son he'd sent him back to gather in the animals with an instruction to keep a lookout for more riders coming from the north. Now, as he drove the big oxen up towards the barn, Felipe could see them, counting four as they came into view, half a mile away along the riverbank. Oxen were big and strong but had only one lumbering pace, so he left them behind as he ran home to get the message to his father. He was surprised to see the stranger with his father; they were going into the barn when Felipe reached them. He pointed along the river to where the group of riders could be clearly seen.

Tom cursed. It wouldn't be possible to return to Sally Locke without being seen by Willis and his men. He would have to remain at the ferry and hope that Sally kept out of sight until they'd gone. He went inside the barn, retrieved Charlie Fairfax's pistol and looked around for somewhere to hide it before Willis and his men arrived. He didn't want to leave it in the barn, didn't want the ferryman implicated in the deputy's death by its accidental discovery so, with time running short, he pushed it into one of the packs on his mule's back. When he stepped out into the daylight the posse was slowing to a walk as they neared Enrique Domingo.

'Look who's here,' Lou Currier said when he espied Tom Belman.

Andrew Willis had no words for Tom, merely a look of haughty superiority.

'Where's my deputy?' he asked Enrique.

The ferryman shrugged and spread his arms in that hopeless, deferential manner adopted by many of his nation when speaking to Americans.

'There is no one else here, señor.'

Willis looked around the assembled buildings as if expecting Charlie Fairfax to step forward and prove Enrique a liar.

'Not here,' he said eventually. 'Where has he gone?'

Enrique gave another shrug. 'No one has been,' he said, then, indicating Tom, added, 'only this man.'

Willis turned his attention to Tom Belman.

'Fairfax and you must have covered the same territory. Did you see him?'

'No. I haven't seen anyone since burying a man you left hanging back there on the range.' Tom didn't disguise the venom in his tone but while he spoke his hand rested on the butt of his pistol, a movement that didn't escape the attention of Andrew Willis. 'What you did back there,' Tom told him, 'was unjustified. I'm just making sure you don't have thoughts along those lines here.'

Lou Currier shifted slowly in his saddle. Tom snapped at him.

'Keep your hands on the saddle horn, Lou.'

Currier grinned. 'I was just gonna suggest to Mr Willis that perhaps Charlie's horse gave out on him, that it was tuckered before we parted ways.'

Willis was less sympathetic.

'More likely he's asleep somewhere.' He turned and spoke to one of the deputies while pointing at the high escarpment. 'Curtis, get up there. Take a look around. Even if he's walking, Fairfax shouldn't be far away.'

Curtis Kennedy rode away, passing out of sight behind the main building where the trail led up from the riverbank to the rocky crags above. Those down below saw him pause on the rim, then spur his horse forward and disappear from sight.

Andrew Willis dismounted and made a sign for Lou Currier and Jim Bolton to do likewise.

'You got coffee,' he said to the ferryman. It was more of a demand than an enquiry. Domingo pointed towards the building that was his home. As they headed in that direction Willis spoke to him again.

'Anyone crossed the river today?'

'*Sí*.'

'A girl?'

'*Sí*.'

'Did you recognize her?'

'*Sí*. She brings the newspapers from Amarillo.'

'Was she alone?'

'*Sí, señor*. She arrived early and was in a hurry to get across the river.'

'How long since you took her across?'

'Four hours. Perhaps more.'

Lou Currier spoke. 'We've got no chance of catching her before she reaches Amarillo and the sheriff there isn't going to hand her over to us. We need to get back to Ortega Point and figure out what to do next.'

'I don't need you to tell me what to do,' Willis told him.

'She's bound to tell her story to the authorities over there. We can't hang around. There are the Rangers to consider.'

'Be quiet,' Willis told him, looking around anxiously in case Tom Belman was close enough to overhear. The drifter was a problem, one that should have been dealt with when their trails first crossed. Now the man was keeping his hand on his gun to let them know he wouldn't be taken by surprise. If they killed him here they would have to kill the ferryman and his boy, too.

'Curtis is in a hurry,' Jim Bolton observed as the other deputy came over the ridge almost recklessly, urging his mount down the slope.

'I found Charlie,' Curtis Kennedy announced, flinging an arm back, pointing at the land beyond the escarpment. 'He's dead. Shot between the eyes. I saw his killer in the distance.'

'Did you recognize him?' asked Lou Currier.

There wasn't a lot of conviction in Curtis Kennedy's voice when he gave his reply.

'Reckon it could have been the girl.'

'No,' Lou told him, 'she's long gone.'

Willis turned his attention to Enrique Domingo, wondering if the ferryman had told him the truth and clearly promising retribution if he'd been lied to.

'Who else had reason to kill Fairfax?' he asked aloud, the question directed at no one in particular.

'Perhaps the kid hadn't been playing a lone hand when he got the Locke girl out of town,' Currier suggested, but the possibility of an accomplice in Ortega Point didn't seem to be his biggest worry. When he spoke again it was to re-stress their need to get out of the territory as quickly as possible. 'We need to gather up the equipment and get out of Texas before the Rangers come calling.'

There was a moment before anyone quitted the landing site when guns could have spat lead and men could have died. Andrew Willis tried hard to maintain an impassive expression as he looked down upon Tom Belman, but there was such a fiery coldness in the traveller's eyes that Willis's distrust of the man, the need for assurance that what he'd witnessed in the gully would never be revealed, couldn't be disguised. Killing the saddle tramp would satisfy his needs but when they looked at each other eye to eye it was apparent that it wouldn't be achieved without an exchange of gunshots, neither would he, Willis, be the former soldier's first target. Lou Currier had already vouched for the fact that Tom Belman had survived battles in which hundreds had been killed. Clearly he wouldn't flinch from pulling the trigger on anyone who threatened him.

Willis spurred his horse forward and led the deputies on to the trail leading up to the escarpment. Lou Currier sat for a moment, a grin on his face that was more threat than friendliness. He stretched out his arm, indicating some point behind Tom Belman. Tom ignored it, kept his eyes on Lou Currier and his hand on his gun.

Currier laughed. 'I don't need to trick you, Tom,' he said. 'Reckon I can outshoot you if I need to.'

'Perhaps, but I'm not leading men into battle so I have no need to turn my back on you.'

Currier straightened in the saddle, the expression on his face hardening, the name of Captain Blayney unspoken but vivid between them. A moment of silence passed before Currier spoke.

'When you cross the river keep heading west. Don't go spreading tales in Amarillo. Don't do anything that makes me come looking for you.' He turned the horse's head and rode off in pursuit of his comrades.

Tom Belman kept his hand on his gun until Lou Currier reached the ridge and was gone from sight.

5

The vague hope entertained by Tom Belman, that Curtis Kennedy's sighting of a distant rider had been some kind of mirage, was soon shattered. As soon as it was practicable to do so, when he was certain that Willis and his men had reached the grasslands and were no longer interested in events at the riverside, Tom had ridden up to the high ground in search of Sally Locke. All he found was the body of Charlie Fairfax, abandoned by his friends, left to feed the beasts that roamed and the birds that were already beginning to circle over that place.

Sally Locke wasn't there; impelled, he supposed, by her desire for justice for Cal Tumbrel she had gone back to Ortega Point. What she hoped to find was unclear to him but he feared for her safety if she meant to resume her search of Andrew Willis's office. Such an undertaking was likely to end up with her in more trouble than she'd been in before being rescued by her young friend. The journey to Ortega Point was several hours' hard ride on a fresh horse and, although he reckoned her mount to be better rested than those of the men in pursuit, he wasn't convinced that that would give her time enough to achieve anything before they caught up with her.

That he too would head for Ortega Point was never in doubt. Any thoughts of foolhardiness on the young woman's part or fear for his own safety never surfaced. He was still bound by the vow he'd made to himself to see her safely back to Amarillo. Tom's opinion that the matter would be better handled by the Texas Rangers hadn't altered; they had the authority and the skill to deal with any and all offences that had been committed by Andrew Willis and his men. By her action, Sally Locke had, for the moment, taken away the option of crossing the river to seek aid from Amarillo. The probability was that she would need help much sooner than it could be mustered by anyone there.

Two factors provided Tom with a glimmer of hope that the posse wouldn't find Sally before he reached Ortega Point. First, they didn't know it was Sally whom they were chasing; to the best of their knowledge she was making tracks along the other side of the Canadian; second, it would be dark when she reached town; if she acted with caution it would be possible to avoid detection.

Enrique Domingo agreed with Tom that the Rangers should be involved in the affair but understood the American's decision to return to Ortega Point. He didn't want any harm to come to Sally Locke but he knew that her being a woman wouldn't provide her with any protection from a ruthless man like Andrew Willis. He agreed to keep the mule in his stable until Tom's return.

★ ★ ★

Jim Bolton's animal was almost on its knees when he tugged on the reins for it to halt. It was lathered with sweat and the heat from its body was rising in malodorous waves.

'He can't go on,' Jim yelled to the two riders ahead, who reined in to look back.

Curtis Kennedy, who had been ten yards behind, stopped his own cayuse alongside Jim Bolton's. After sliding out of the saddle he too declared his horse incapable of running any further without a rest. It staggered slightly, then stretched out its neck as though struggling to get air into is lungs. Curtis undid the cinch straps and took the weight of the saddle off its back.

Andrew Willis studied the scene. It was three hours since they'd left the river and they'd covered a lot of ground. The trail of Charlie Fairfax's killer wasn't difficult to see but it didn't need a Paiute tracker to know where it would lead. There was no point in riding the horses to death; they were all heading for Ortega Point. Besides, Willis thought, the usefulness of these men had expired with his greater need to flee the state. His horse had the stamina to get him back to his farm but these men could remain here until they were gathered up by the Rangers for all he cared.

'No point killing the animals,' he said. 'I'll meet you in town tomorrow.'

Before he could ride away Lou Currier threw a question.

'What's the plan?'

Willis didn't like the manner of the sheriff's question; he knew it carried a wagonload of distrust. He kept the anger out of his reply and the superiority in his tone.

'I've got some thinking to do,' he confessed. 'We'll discuss what needs to be done tomorrow.' To put an end to the conversation, he kicked his heels against the big chestnut and rode away across the plains.

★ ★ ★

Lou Currier and Andrew Willis had first crossed trails in Missouri some months after the end of war, each looking for easy money and careless of how it was acquired. Willis, a former colonel in the Confederate army, had been reduced to making his money at gambling tables, happy to deal off the bottom or resort to any other trick to ensure that table stakes ended up in his pocket. There were times, however, when his style and false grandeur failed to disguise the cheating and on one such occasion he'd been grateful for the intervention of Lou Currier to get him safely out of town.

Until that night, Currier's activities had been base robbery with menaces and violence. He had been watching the card game with the intention of following the big winner at the end of the night and relieving him of his winnings, but when the character of the man he'd marked out was revealed to be no more honest than his own he'd seen the possibility of achieving more regular paydays. He'd used his guns to get the man out of the gambling saloon and clear of town. He'd demanded half the winnings as payment, then proposed that they should join forces. It was a simple plan: one which required little more of Willis than building up his character as a gentleman gambler. It wasn't even necessary for him to win at the tables; his role was to identify the men with money, the rest became Currier's concern.

The success of the scheme was total but the reward was limited and Andrew Willis was forever on the lookout for riches greater than those that could be acquired by such petty theft.

The answer arrived when Lou Currier met up with a man he'd known during the war. That man was Gary Hudson and the tales he told of his work as a forger for the US government struck the spark that was to become the flame of Willis's ambition. Willis and Currier rented a farm in the Texas panhandle for the centre of their operation. It provided routes for the distribution of counterfeit notes as well as one into the uncharted western territories, where a man could escape the clutches of the law in an emergency.

Now an emergency had arisen.

★ ★ ★

As Lou Currier watched the other man ride into the darkening east suspicion filled his mind. Despite their shared crimes the trust between the two men was tenuous but they understood each other. Willis's haste to put distance between them sent a clear message: it was every man for himself. Currier pulled the ears of his horse.

'I reckon this one'll carry me to town,' he told Kennedy and Bolton. 'I'll see you two at the jail in the morning.'

He swung the horse and set course for Ortega Point.

For the last few miles before reaching
the outskirts of town the pace of Sally
Locke's filly dropped. This wasn't
entirely due to weariness, although the
horse had gamely covered the ground
with the benefit of only one ten-minute
respite. The loss of daylight also
contributed to the reduced speed. It
also made redundant the glances over
her shoulder that she had cast fre-
quently during her ride. At no time as
she'd covered the grassland had she
seen any sign of pursuit and now the
trail was well defined, confirming that
she was approaching the nearby settlement. Her thoughts shifted from the
nagging fear of pursuit to devising a
plan of action upon reaching Ortega
Point.

Evading Sheriff Currier and his
deputies remained her top priority, so
she didn't want to arouse any interest in
the town by clattering along Main
Street, which would be alive with the

usual crowd of citizens who frequented the night-time streets. She would be recognized and news of her precipitate arrival would spread throughout the town in a matter of minutes.

Furthermore, apart from the dead Charlie Fairfax, she didn't know the identities of the men riding with Willis and Currier. It was possible that either Curtis Kennedy or Jim Bolton had remained in town. If so, and they got wind of her return, they would know that her target would be Willis's office.

She considered circling the town to stable her horse in the livery at the far end of Main Street. Perhaps she would get there unobserved, enabling her to get the animal off the street before it could be seen and remarked upon by everyone, but there was no guarantee that the stableman wouldn't gossip or, indeed, wasn't paid by Willis or the sheriff to report unusual arrivals. Since that pair had arrived in town Ortega Point had become a less friendly place.

Her reflections brought to mind people like Mrs Pinder, Doctor Carter and Sam Dack. It was then that she remembered the barn at the rear of Sam Dack's home. Everyone knew of his readiness to make money and that he'd housed travellers and their animals in the past. She knew the filly would be safe in Sam's barn; when she'd spoken to him two days earlier it had been apparent that he was no friend of Sheriff Currier or Andrew Willis. That had been one of the reasons she'd pretended she wanted him to be a reporter for Ortega Point's own journal: she'd known he'd keep a critical eye on anything that involved those men.

At that time of day activity was concentrated around the two saloons and the Texas Hotel in the middle of Main Street. Confident that her arrival had not aroused any interest, she dismounted at the head of the street and walked her horse into the alley that led to the barn at the rear of Sam Dack's house. The old man, she guessed, would be among those drinking rotgut or beer elsewhere in town. As silently as possible she opened the barn door and led the filly inside.

Sam's two horses were already stabled there and they snuffled as Sally and her filly stepped inside. Even though the barn was virtually out of sight from anyone passing on Main Street she was reluctant to light a lantern. Fortunately, even when the door was closed, a high side window allowed in a small measure of moonlight, which was enough for Sally to work by.

She worked swiftly and as silently as possible, unsaddling her own horse then rubbing it down with handfuls of clean straw. She hunted around until she found a bucket which she scooped into a water butt for the horse to drink from. Tending to the animal's needs aroused her own hunger pangs; she had had neither food nor drink since her early-morning arrival at Domingo's Ferry. She was aware of the emptiness of her stomach but she knew she couldn't delay a search of Andrew Willis's office if she hoped to do it before he and his men returned to town. She hadn't seen any sign of them on her back trail but calculated that they wouldn't be far behind.

Satisfied that her horse was settled, Sally left the barn. She was slipping the retaining bar into its holding sockets when she felt the muzzle of a gun pressed against the back of her neck and a voice sounded hoarsely in her ear.

'What do you think you're doing, young feller?'

A lantern swung somewhere close by, casting her shadow against the barn door.

'Who is it, Sam?' asked a second voice.

'It's me, Mr Dack. Sally Locke.' Sally began to turn slowly to prove the truth of her words. 'I don't mean any harm. Just wanted somewhere safe to leave my horse. I meant to pay you but I didn't think you were at home.'

Sam Dack was slowly lowering his pistol, completely taken by surprise by the identity of his intruder.

'He wasn't at home,' said Doctor Carter, who was holding the lantern. 'We were halfway down the street when we saw you sneak into the alley. There's only Sam's barn back here so we were curious as to what you were up to.'

'I'm sorry,' Sally said. She was anxious to get away, continue with her quest to search Andrew Willis's office, but knew it wasn't going to be easy. The expressions on the men's faces reflected not only bewilderment at her presence but concern over her appearance. Her features weren't just marred by tiredness but were also grubby with sweat and grime. Her clothing, too, was crumpled and soiled and gave off the heavy smell of a well-run horse.

'What are you doing here, girl?' Sam asked. 'I thought you'd returned to Amarillo two days ago.'

'I got held up,' she replied, not

knowing what she should tell these men. She did not doubt that she could trust them but she was unwilling to put them in danger, which was a possibility if they became involved in her need to avenge the death of Cal Tumbrel. 'I need some information for an article my father is preparing.'

'You're not going to find anyone to talk to tonight,' John Carter told her. 'You shouldn't be alone on the streets at this hour, it's not safe.'

'Is there no law in this town?' she asked.

Sam Dack's grunt was an expression of scorn.

'Not much at the best of times but none at all at present. They're all out chasing an escaped prisoner. Come on, we'll take you along to Mrs Pinder's house and get you a bed for the night.'

But Sally skipped away from them; the information that all the law officers were out of town was what she needed to hear. It meant that there wouldn't be a guard on Willis's office. It was the opportunity she needed to conduct a search of that place.

*   *   *

As the evening gloom gathered around him Tom Belman settled his horse into a long-reaching, rhythmical stride which ate away the miles of prairie land that lay between the Canadian River and Ortega Point. It was a pace the sorrel could maintain for long stretches and which suited Tom's needs. He was eager to catch up with the young woman before she found herself in great danger but caution was essential: those who were a threat to her were somewhere between him and wherever she was now, and although he had no reason to suppose that Willis and his men were watching their back trail it was essential that they didn't become aware of his pursuit; he would be of no help to Sally if he fell foul of Willis and his men. Even so, in the fading light he almost missed the thin wisp of smoke that was rising from a knoll less than a mile ahead.

He'd been thinking of the exchange of words he'd had with Lou Currier before the sheriff had climbed the escarpment to catch up with the rest of the bunch. His oblique reference to the death of Captain Blayney and the implied accusation of murder had been out of character for him. He wasn't a man who went looking for trouble and, in truth, he had nothing to back up that imputation other than the itch in his gut every time he thought about it. But Currier had offered no denial. Indeed, if Tom's hand hadn't been resting on the butt of his Colt, it was probable that the sheriff of Ortega Point would have attempted to make Tom another victim. The expression on his face and the words that left his mouth before leaving had made that clear.

The sorrel slithered to a halt, skipped a little dance to regain its balance, then stood perfectly still while awaiting its rider's next instruction. Tom sat as still as the animal, as though the slightest movement would now carry across the grassland and betray his location to those gathered around the fire. He eased himself out of the saddle and ran a hand along the sorrel's neck, a gesture of reassurance that relaxed the animal.

It was possible, he knew, that the people who had made camp at this spot had nothing to do with Willis and the posse. They could be travellers heading in any direction who had picked this place as a suitable night camp; its features weren't dissimilar to the place he had himself chosen the previous night. If that were the case he could ride on; his passing wouldn't be of any interest to those camped on the knoll, but the concern expressed by the deputies earlier in the day regarding the capability of their horses was also in his mind.

Perhaps they'd been forced to abandon the attempt to catch their unknown prey and plans were being made to flee from Ortega Point before the Texas Rangers arrived. Their belief that Sally Locke had crossed the river meant that such a tactic could be large in their thinking. How would they react if they heard him ride by? Would they be sufficiently concerned to attempt to ride him down? Could he emulate Cal Tumbrel: be a decoy to drag them away from town, so giving Sally Locke time enough to find evidence that Andrew Willis was the source of the counterfeit money?

Tom wasn't prepared to leave the question to chance. He needed to know the truth of the matter. If the men in the camp were strangers then he would hurry on to Ortega Point to find the young woman; if not he needed to find a means of delaying them before riding into town.

Leading the sorrel by the bridle, he made his way forward, quickly at first but with increasing circumspection the nearer he got to the knoll. Fifty yards from the knoll Tom ground-hitched the horse. He could see the fire's glow and small flickers of flame that flashed now and then through the foliage of low bushes. He couldn't see any movement but he dropped to the ground and began to crawl in case a lookout had been posted. As he worked his way up the knoll he drew his gun, ready to protect himself should the need arise. At the top he found a point that provided tree cover and gave him a moment to study the scene.

To his left a rope had been slung between a tree and a spindly bush, five yards apart, forming a picket line to which the horses were tied, but there were only two mounts, not the four he would have expected if the campers were Willis and his followers. He remained cautious, however, staying low to the ground lest he startled the horses and they snickered a warning to their riders, but the animals remained motionless, still enough to seem asleep on their feet.

Above the crackle of burning twigs

Tom could hear a low murmur of voices. He moved to his right, away from the animals, and circled behind the men who were lounging against their saddles, smoke rising from the cigarettes they held between their fingers.

Recognition of the deputies who had been at the ferry crossing with Lou Currier rewarded Tom for his caution. He wondered where the other two were, wondered if Willis and Currier were close and likely to join these two soon, but that possibility was soon cleared from his mind after he'd listened to a few sentences of the conversation. Curtis Kennedy was close to anger, trying to get Jim Bolton to admit that he too suspected they'd been duped by Willis and Currier.

'They won't be in Ortega Point when we get there tomorrow,' prophesied Kennedy. 'They've left us to face the Rangers.'

Jim Bolton's reply sounded like nothing more than a non-committal grunt to Tom. Curtis Kennedy spoke again.

'They'll share the money and we'll get nothing.'

'What can we do about it?'

'Nothing while we're stuck out here.'

'You want to follow them?'

'On what?' Tom could hear the sneer in Kennedy's retort. 'Those animals are so exhausted they won't be able to travel before midday tomorrow. Even then they'll be capable of little more than walking pace.'

'So what do we do?'

Curtis Kennedy flicked the stub of his cigarette towards the campfire.

'Nothing we can do at the moment. Get back to Ortega Point as soon as possible.'

'But you don't expect them to be there? Perhaps we should avoid the town. Make tracks into the north country where the Rangers can't touch us.'

Curtis Kennedy agreed with his companion; fleeing Texas had become a priority. Although rankled by the belief that Willis and Currier intended to run off with their money, he and Bolton couldn't risk being in Ortega Point when the Rangers arrived. Not only had they been responsible for the girl's imprisonment but they'd been involved, too, in the lynching out on the prairie. If that was ever discovered they would be shown no pity. But, as he explained to Bolton, they needed first to return to town.

'We need fresh horses, Jim. Where else will we get them? If Willis and Currier have fled then we hightail it, too. We'll track them down and get what we're owed. We can't do that if we're in prison.'

'What about the Rangers?'

'We have a head start on them. The Rangers aren't likely to get to Ortega Point until late tomorrow. Nobody else can stop us.'

'*I can.*' Tom Belman's voice was soft but that didn't lessen the threat it carried.

The deputies twisted, reaching for their side guns but quickly realizing the futility of such a move. Tom's gun was already in his hand and covering any offensive move that they might make.

'You!' exclaimed Curtis Kennedy.

'Yes, me. Now, one at a time, throw your guns over here.'

Under Tom's direction, Curtis Kennedy was first to obey the instruction, then Jim Bolton followed suit. Tom kicked the weapons aside, under a bush.

'What do you intend to do with us?' Jim Bolton asked.

It was a question that troubled Tom. He couldn't hang around until their horses were fit enough to travel: getting to Sally demanded greater urgency. He was reluctant to tie them up and leave them in this place but he had no other option. If anything happened to him they might never be found and die of thirst or starvation.

'The government calls it treason to counterfeit money,' he said. 'You'll hang for it if found guilty.' In the firelight he could see Jim Bolton cast an anxious look at Curtis Kennedy.

'We didn't print it,' he told Tom.

'I don't really care about that,' Tom replied. 'I want to see you punished for killing young Cal Tumbrel. That was murder done to cover up the counterfeiting. You'll hang for that, too. Now, come over here. You first.' He pointed at Bolton with the barrel of his gun.

Reluctantly, nervously, Jim Bolton stood and walked forward. When he was five yards away Tom ordered him to remove his belt. When Bolton had handed it over Tom used it to secure its owner's hands behind his back. It was only the first step in binding them. When he had the hands of both men fastened he would get a saddle rope and tie them up more securely. He pushed Jim Bolton to the ground and turned his attention to Curtis Kennedy.

'Now you,' he called.

Curtis put his hands on his saddle to push himself upright. For a moment he appeared to stumble: then, when he completed the movement, Tom saw that he had a rifle in his hand. Instantly, it spat flame and lead. Two bullets passed close to Tom but they'd been fired too quickly to have any accuracy.

Tom fired off two rounds of his own before moving towards the protection of the tree to his left. To avoid Tom's bullets Curtis had dived to the ground and taken refuge behind his saddle. Jim Bolton shouted out to Curtis the direction in which Tom was heading. Tom fired twice more, reversed the direction he had been moving in and swiped the barrel of his gun across the bound deputy's brow as he passed him. Then he dived low, rolled and reached the relative safety of the tree. There he paused, ejected the four spent shells and replaced them with cartridges from his gunbelt. He waited for Curtis to make the next move.

'Where is he, Jim?' Curtis called, but Jim was unconscious and unable to reply. It had been a bad call, letting

Tom know that his opponent was unsure of his location.

It had given Tom an advantage that he now made use of by squirming across the ground and over the side of the knoll, where Curtis couldn't see him. He progressed around the knoll with cautious haste, keeping an eye on the ridge in case the deputy was attempting a similar ruse, but when he heard him calling to his partner again he felt assured that he hadn't moved. When he calculated that he'd reached a point that had him behind his enemy Tom climbed to the top again.

With the fire behind it, Curtis Kennedy had put his hat on a stick, attempting to set up a target that would draw Tom's fire from the far cover where he supposed him to be.

'I'm here,' Tom told him, speaking from behind and making it clear that he had the upper hand.

Curtis's frame stiffened momentarily, then relaxed. It seemed that he accepted the fact that he could no longer win a shoot-out. Swiftly he twisted, rolling off his belly to face the man behind. He swung his rifle in an arc that was never completed. Before he could pull the trigger Tom had fired twice. Curtis Kennedy died where he lay.

When Tom rode away he left Jim Bolton unconscious and tied up with his own belt. It was probable that the deputy would work free of the bindings before anyone found him and, with the threat of the gallows to spur his flight, would probably flee from the territory. Tom rued the likelihood of the deputy escaping punishment for the killing of Cal Tumbrel but he wasn't in a position to prevent it. He couldn't afford to lose any more time; finding Sally Locke was more important.

He hoped she'd been able to avoid the clutches of Lou Currier and Andrew Willis.

6

When Lou Currier reached Ortega Point it was without any expectation of finding Andrew Willis there. If his partner had had flight in mind then he didn't expect him to waste time in that town.

The office along Main Street had been a sham: a front to establish respectability and influence as though he was a bona fide businessman. A couple of deals had been brokered in that office, giving Willis control of a couple of small businesses. They had been legitimate transactions even if they had been financed by illegally obtained money. With regard to the counterfeiting operation, there was nothing in the office that would incriminate Willis, Currier or anyone else. All of that business had been conducted out at the farm and it was to that place that

Currier assumed Willis had gone. He would have cut east long before he reached the outskirts of town.

Currier acknowledged that the success of the counterfeiting scheme was due mainly to Andrew Willis's control of it. From its inception, after Willis had first been introduced to Gary Hudson, the plan and the requirements to fulfil it had seemed to be complete in his brain. Like the officer he'd been during the war, he'd planned, organized and commanded without a thought of failure.

Seeing the opportunity to accumulate great wealth he had set about the task with considerable fervour. He had selected the small Texas town as the base of operations, organized the materials and equipment essential to produce perfect copies and had established links throughout the neighbouring states for the distribution of the forged notes. It seemed that overnight he had transformed himself from a disreputable gambler into a person of consequence. In a short time his recommendation to appoint Lou as sheriff had been acted upon, putting him in a position to gain early warning of official investigations that might threaten their enterprise.

Lou, however, was not forgetting that they had been equal partners in the past and he saw no reason for that to change. Willis had adopted the role of Grand Panjandrum but in Currier's opinion that was simply for public consumption. In private they were still equal partners: if Andrew Willis entertained other ideas then he would learn that Lou's guns did his arguing for him.

Unlike Andrew Willis, he had things in town that he needed to collect before making a run for the border. Among his few possessions was the biggest bankroll he'd ever had. He wasn't prepared to leave that behind. Just as important, however, was his need for a fresh horse, so his first stop was the livery stable at the far end of town.

There was plenty of activity in the vicinity of Queenie's Palace and The

Alamo when Lou Currier clattered along Main Street. A few heads turned in his direction but no one threw a word of greeting. The citizens weren't his greatest admirers but he kept trouble out of town so the councilmen had no cause to remove him from office. All day, speculation over the identity of the escaped prisoner had been rife but unresolved. The return of the sheriff, alone, implied that the man had not been recaptured. No one would speak of it in case their enquiry carried a suggestion of failure. Sheriff Currier didn't like criticism.

Horses were hitched at rails all along the street and Lou Currier cast an eye over them as he rode past. He wasn't sure how far ahead Charlie Fairfax's killer had been, how long he'd been in town, but he figured the horse he'd ridden would be easy to recognize. Lou's own was sagging now and streaked with white lines of sweat. As he slowed it to a walk its breath steamed in the night air. Lou didn't see another in similar condition all the way to the stable.

At the big double doors he climbed down and led the tired animal inside.

'I'm going out again in an hour,' he told the night ostler. 'Put my saddle on the best horse available.' He looked at the animals in the stalls and pointed at a black gelding. 'That one, and I need another to carry a pack.'

The ostler took the tired horse and began to unsaddle it.

'Anyone else left their horse here in the last hour?' the sheriff asked.

'Not in the last hour. A couple of strangers rode in earlier from Kansas. Their horses are in the back stalls.' The ostler waved an arm to indicate the far end of the building.

Lou Currier examined them but was quickly satisfied that they hadn't been subjected to the same sort of run that his own had endured. He left the stable, going off in the direction of the Texas Hotel where the town provided his accommodation.

*   *   *

Two nights earlier Sally Locke had found a window with a faulty catch at the back of Andrew Willis's office through which she had gained access to the premises. Because of the need to pursue her to the Canadian River, the necessary repair to that catch had not been undertaken and she was able to raise the lower section and climb inside again. This time her activities weren't under scrutiny and she was able to conduct the search that had earlier been prevented by the intervention of Charlie Fairfax and the other deputies.

Once inside the building Sally worked quickly although with no little trepidation. Rather than being reassured by the absence of other people, she found that the silence and darkness by which she was surrounded seemed to press around her body, tightening her chest and making it difficult to breathe. This time, aware of the ruthlessness of which Willis and his men were capable, the risk of discovery held a greater threat. Despite the cool night-time temperature her brow was damp with sweat. Her mouth was dry and she needed to work her tongue to generate enough saliva to make it easier to swallow. When she did she was able to let go of the breath she'd been holding, allow her muscles to relax, which set her free to begin her investigation.

She went from the back room into the front office where there was a desk and a cupboard to search. The lack of light was a handicap and she knew it would be difficult to examine the documents she found. She wasn't prepared to run the risk of discovery by lowering the blind and lighting the lamp on the desk. The smallest glimmer could alert someone to an intruder and she had no real reason for being in Andrew Willis's office. However, right outside the office, one of the kerosene lamps that lit up the street hung on a high nail. The dull, yellow glow it cast was barely adequate for Sally's purpose but it was the best light available. Piece by piece, she took what she found in the desk over to the window so that she could examine them by the lamp's dim illumination.

In fact, there was very little documentation to inspect and what she found was unconnected with any nefarious act. Documents endorsed by the lawyer, Jonathon Bartlett, showed that Andrew Willis had some interest in, or control of, three of the town's long-established businesses but, whether or not that information was general knowledge around Ortega Point, there was nothing to imply his involvement was anything but genuine business transactions. She found nothing that linked him to the forgeries of which she supposed him guilty; no ink, no linen paper, no printing plates or machinery, and definitely no bundles of money: not a single bill.

Disappointed, she reopened the back window and climbed out into the darkness of the rear alley. She pressed herself against the building and waited a moment to acclimatize herself to the night and listen for activity on Main Street in case there was anyone in the vicinity of Willis's office. Content that it was safe to proceed, she moved forward. She had covered only two steps when a rough hand reached from behind, covered her mouth and pulled her back into the building's dark shadow. Sally tried to struggle free but her attacker's other arm had encircled her waist and she found herself lifted off the ground. She was turned and slammed against the wall; her head collided heavily with stout timbers, dazing her; her legs were barely able to keep her upright when she was set down on her feet.

Lou Currier looked at the young woman with amazement. While passing the office on his route from the livery stable to the Texas Hotel he'd glimpsed a movement at the window, an ethereal motion that could have been a reflection of someone on the board-walk or the flicker of the kerosene lamp in distorted glass, but there hadn't been anyone on that part of the street nor any wind to disturb a flame. He'd paused, watched and seen again the spectre-like vision. Lou Currier didn't believe in ghosts. He'd waited in the alley to catch the intruder but when he'd done so he hadn't expected it to be the Amarillo newspaper-owner's daughter.

'You,' he said, gripping her upper arms and shaking her violently so that between that rough treatment and the blow to the head she was unable to summon up the ability to shout out her plight. For Currier, her presence in Ortega Point put a different complex-ion on the situation. She wasn't the threat that he and Willis had considered her to be but he couldn't allow her to roam free around town to stir up trouble. Willis wanted to be the decision maker, he thought, so let him decide what was to be done with her. He needed to get her out to the farm without anyone's knowledge, and the first priority in maintaining secrecy was to keep her quiet. Without another word he punched her hard on the jaw. She collapsed on to the ground, completely unconscious.

As a temporary measure he used his own and Sally's bandannas to gag and bind her hands, then he rolled Sally into the darkest part of the alley and hoped that no one would find her before he returned. He meant to return to the livery stable and have the spare horse hitched to a buggy so that he could get the young woman out of town unobserved. When he left the alley, however, he saw the doctor and the town's windbag on the far side of the street, scratching their heads as though puzzling over one of the world's great mysteries. In a popularity contest he doubted if he would get the vote of either man, but neither was likely to impede the maintenance of town law. He hailed them as he crossed the street and explained his need.

Doctor Carter said he wasn't anyone's errand boy and moved on up the street towards Queenie's Palace. A flipped dollar coin, however, won over Sam Dack. The suddenness of Sally Locke's disappearance troubled him but he was able, temporarily, to supplant that concern with his long-held belief that if there was a dollar to be made it was better made by him than anyone else.

'Leave the buggy in that alley when you return,' Currier told him, then stood for a moment to watch the old-timer as he hurried off towards the stable.

Ten minutes later the buggy was parked at the edge of the alley with the black horse saddled and tethered to its back rail. Lou Currier waited a few moments to ensure that there was no one in the vicinity then rebound the woman more securely. This time he used the saddle rope, discarding the more flimsy material of the bandannas.

Although she was unlikely to work herself free, he was keen to forestall any attempt to do so. When he lifted her into the buggy she moaned slightly, a sign that she was beginning to regain consciousness. He threw a rug over her to hide her from curious eyes, then climbed into the seat and slapped the reins to urge the horse into motion.

* * *

Tom Belman saw the silhouette of a buggy heading east when he was half a mile from Ortega Point but had no reason to suppose that it was being driven by Lou Currier, nor that a sore and groggy Sally Locke was lying on its floor. He completed his ride and, as Sally had done less than an hour earlier, made his way to the back of Sam Dack's house to stable his tired horse. He wanted it off the street; a weary, sweating horse was likely to draw attention and would, perhaps, be recognized by Lou Currier. Tom hoped to find Sally without alerting the sheriff to the fact that either of them had returned to town.

Tom had used the barn during his stay in Ortega Point and, knowing Sam's eagerness to make a dollar here and there, figured he'd be welcome to use it again. He lit a lamp and worked quickly to unsaddle and settle the sorrel. Then, as he was slinging his harness over a rail, he noticed the other tired animal in the barn and recognized it immediately. The knowledge that Sally had reached town safely provided confirmation that he'd judged her intention correctly. Now he had to find her and get her safely to her home across the Canadian. Sam Dack, he thought, might know where to find her.

Sam wasn't at home but that didn't surprise Tom, it was the old-timer's custom at this time of night to join his friend Doctor Carter in Queenie's Palace or The Alamo. Without making himself conspicuous, Tom worked his way along the street, evading, wherever possible, the direct glow from the streetlamps. Andrew Willis and Lou Currier, he suspected, were somewhere in Ortega Point. If they saw him it wouldn't be to his advantage.

When he reached The Alamo, he paused, leant against the wall beside the long window and peered in. It wasn't a big room and although it was full of smoke it didn't take much time for Tom to assure himself that the man he was looking for wasn't within. He moved on and, as before, advanced carefully. On a couple of occasions he found it necessary to take evasive action, darting into an alley, to avoid meeting, face to face, men who, judging by their physique or manner of walking, might have been Lou Currier. But he reached Queenie's Palace without discovery.

Sam Dack and Doctor Carter had their backs to the swing doors and their heads together as they leant side by side against a counter that was little more than waist high. From his observation point at the doorway, Tom Belman knew that he would only get Sam's attention by joining him at the bar. Before pushing open the batwings he took stock of the saloon's customers and satisfied himself that there was no one within who had any reason to be watching for him. His entrance didn't arouse more than casual interest; here and there a head turned to follow his progress but the gaze latched on to him for no more than a step or two before turning back to the cards, whiskey or companion that had been momentarily forsaken.

Tom shrugged a place for himself alongside Sam Dack.

'Hey, young feller,' said the surprised old-timer when he recognized his former boarder, 'what are you doing here? Thought you'd be halfway to the Sierras by now.' He chuckled at his own exaggeration. He turned to the doctor and shook his head to indicate his astonishment. 'What's going on in this town tonight, John?'

'I need to speak to you,' Tom said.

He looked around pointedly at those who were gathered near by. He had no reason to suppose they were there to overhear his conversation but Sally Locke's safety was in jeopardy and he wasn't prepared to take any risks. 'Let's step outside,' he suggested and to forestall any unnecessary discussion by the garrulous old-timer, he walked away from the bar. Sam and the doctor joined him on the street a few moments later.

'I put my horse in your barn . . . ' Tom began.

'Sure. Do you want a bed, too?'

Tom waved the question aside. 'Sally Locke's horse was in there,' he said.

'Her turning up was as much of a surprise as your coming back. Thought she'd gone back to Amarillo a couple of days ago.'

'Where is she now?'

'I don't know. Nearly shot her for a horse thief, then she just vanished. Left us scratching our heads. Ain't that right, Doc?'

John Carter confirmed Sam's words.

'Sally said she was seeking some information for her father. We wanted to walk her to Mrs Pinder's rooming house but she disappeared into the night. We haven't seen her since.'

Tom Belman cursed. 'Sally could be in danger,' he told his companions. 'She's not seeking information for her father, she's trying to prove that Andrew Willis is responsible for the counterfeit money that is currently circulating.' He related the events that had befallen him since leaving Ortega Point the previous day.

'They hanged the boy?' Sam uttered the words with a mixture of disbelief and sadness.

'And I suspect they'll kill Sally, too, if they catch her,' Tom explained, 'which is why I need to find her and get her home. My guess is that she came here to search Andrew Willis's office before he got back to town. But he and Lou Currier were ahead of me. They should be here now.'

'The sheriff!' Sam Dack spat on the ground. 'I've just done that sonofabitch a favour.' His fingers fiddled in the small pocket of his old vest and extracted a dollar piece. Wordlessly, he drew back his arm then threw the coin into the blackness of the night, as far down the street as his strength permitted.

'What kind of favour?' Tom wanted to know.

The answer, when it came, prickled his senses. He was sure that the sudden need for a buggy was significant, that somehow it had been instigated by Sally Locke, and that feeling was intensified when Sam further informed him that he'd left the buggy in the alley beside Andrew Willis's office.

Surreptitiously the three of them crossed the street to investigate the office. The doors at front and back were locked and all the windows secured. Although he was sure the building was empty Tom tapped lightly on the rear windows and softly called Sally's name.

If she was still within the building he hoped she would recognize his voice and open the door. When nothing happened the men retraced their steps to Main Street. Talk of a buggy recalled the memory of the distant silhouette he'd seen when approaching town. He mentioned it to Sam.

'That would be the sheriff,' the old-timer confirmed, 'probably going to the Willis farm about five miles east of here.'

Doctor Carter, who had been lagging a few steps behind the other two, gave a shout.

'What've you got?' asked Sam. John Carter held up a length of yellow cloth.

'It's a bandanna,' he replied.

Tom took the piece of cloth from the medical man and ran it through his fingers, slowly, as though subjecting it to a minute examination, but that was hardly necessary. He knew he'd seen it around Sally Locke's neck.

'They've got her,' he said. 'Sally is their prisoner again.'

7

The buggy driven by Lou Currier bumped and rattled its way over the hard-baked clay and slewed to an abrupt halt in front of the farmhouse. At this hour of the day it was rare for men to be active about the place, those who hadn't ridden five miles to partake of the pleasures on offer in Ortega Point were usually found around a table with a pack of cards or perusing magazines and catalogues with pictures to be discussed, cut out and pasted on the bunkhouse walls. But Lou wasn't surprised to observe the activity that was in progress this night.

Lights were aglow in the far barn where the printing machine was housed but he was certain that no false money was currently being produced. In fact, the work under way, he guessed, was to put an end to the generation of ten-dollar bills. The machine was being dismantled, the parts and materials were being spread among different wagon loads for reassembly when another safe location was found.

Lou's arrival had not gone unnoticed; 'Kansas' Bill Kirkup, who had drawn guard duty, had been patrolling near the gate when he'd caught the sound of the fast-approaching buggy. His warning to the men in the barn had caused them to cease their activity briefly, but they had resumed again when the new arrival was identified. Lou was tying the buggy-puller to a hitching post, where a white, nervous horse was already tethered, when a round-shouldered, bow-legged man bustled across to him from the barn. He looked concerned.

'What's going on, Lou?' he asked.

'Got you dismantling the press, eh?'

Gary Hudson nodded.

'He's expecting the Rangers to come a-raiding,' Lou told him.

The explanation startled his former army comrade.

'The Texas Rangers?'

The reputation of that outfit scared every law-breaker in the state.

'Relax,' Lou told him. 'Willis is jumping at shadows. It's not going to happen — at least, not any time soon.' He pointed at the buggy. 'I've got some baggage in there that will ease his mind. Bring it in.' He climbed on to the veranda but before opening the door he spoke again to Gary Hudson. 'Careful it doesn't bite you.' He grinned, then went inside the farmhouse.

Andrew Willis wasn't in the big room where the men congregated at night and ate their meals during the day, but there was a smaller room behind it: a private place that he used as an office. Other people entered there only when they were invited. It was, therefore, with anger and alarm that he looked up from his desk when the door was abruptly opened. Lou Currier leaned against the jamb, studying Willis, his steely-eyed glance informing the other that he'd anticipated his plan to flee with the greater part of the profits.

On the desk were stacks of money: old bills, indicating that they were genuine currency, and four small objects wrapped in strips of blanket material for their protection. These, Lou Currier suspected, were the plates from which the counterfeit money was printed. Andrew Willis was in the process of placing them carefully into one pouch of a well-used saddle-bag.

'What are you doing here?' Willis asked.

'What? You thought I meant to stay out on the prairie with my deputies? That would have been convenient for you, wouldn't it. But no, I know you, Willis. Perhaps you've conveniently forgotten that we're partners but I haven't. Even if you have fooled everybody in town and convinced yourself that you're a big shot I know you for the mediocre gambler that you are. Trying to leave here with my share of the money would be a gamble you'd definitely lose.' Lou drummed the tips of his fingers on the butt of his revolver to emphasize the point.

'I had no such thoughts,' said Andrew Willis, but the lie showed in his eyes.

'The saddled white out there tells a different story.'

'I was going to take a room at the Texas Hotel so that I'd be in town when you arrived.'

'Don't waste your flimflam on me. You're scared of the Rangers and mean to get out of the state before morning. I suppose those are the plates that you've wrapped up so carefully.' Currier indicated the small bundle in Willis's hand. 'Doesn't matter what else you lose or who else gets caught as long as you hang on to the most essential item for printing money.'

'What do you want me to do, leave them here for the Rangers to find? With these in their possession nowhere would be safe for us. We've committed a federal crime. Our names and descriptions would be relayed across the nation. Lawmen in every state would be on the lookout for us. I'm taking a risk for the good of everyone else.'

Lou Currier grinned, mocking Willis's false nobility, but at that moment noises could be heard in the big room behind Lou.

'Perhaps you don't need to sacrifice yourself; it might not be necessary to dismantle the set-up we have here.'

'What do you mean?'

'I've brought you a present.'

Before Willis could make any response Gary Hudson opened the door and shoved Sally Locke into the room with such force that she stumbled, lost her balance and landed awkwardly in a heap on the floor. Hudson lifted his left leg and rubbed his shin.

'Biting is the only thing she didn't try to do,' he grumbled to Lou Currier.

'Who is this?' asked Andrew Willis.

'This,' the sheriff told him, 'is the girl we rode all the way to the Canadian to find. This is the newspaper-owner's daughter, Sally Locke.'

'You found her out on the prairie?'

'No, I found her in Ortega Point. She'd been searching your office.'

'But she should be in Amarillo.'

'It seems the ferryman lied to us.'

Lou Currier gripped Sally's arm and roughly pulled her to her feet.

'Sit there,' he told her, pushing her on to a high-backed chair at the side of the desk.

'That's the second time you've been caught in my office,' said Andrew Willis. 'What are you looking for?'

Sally didn't answer, merely rubbed her upper arms where the sheriff had gripped them.

'I'm in no mood for games,' Willis told her. 'Tell us what you were doing in my office.'

Sally raised eyes that were bright with defiance. With an open hand Willis slapped her hard across the face, the force of the blow pitching her on to the floor again. When Lou Currier lifted her once more on to the seat she raised a hand involuntarily to her stinging face. She didn't want to show her pain but, when surrounded by three threatening men, it was difficult hide the vulnerability she felt. Her ears were ringing and her eyesight was blurred with moisture. She could hear Andrew Willis's voice but she disregarded the words and had to press her lips tightly together to sustain her resistance.

As she turned her head away from her aggressor her eyes alighted on the wads of money on the desk. Despite her predicament the possibility that she was looking at counterfeit bills flashed into her mind, and the desire to get hold of some of them as evidence of Andrew Willis's guilt revived her resolve.

'Why are you prying into my affairs?' Willis wanted to know. 'Who sent you here?'

Sally lifted her head.

'You have no right to keep me here,' she declared. 'I haven't stolen anything from you. I haven't done anything wrong.'

'Nothing wrong?' scoffed Andrew Willis. 'Breaking into someone else's property might not be a major felony but killing an officer of the law certainly is.'

'What are you talking about?' she asked.

'I'm talking about Charlie Fairfax, Sheriff Currier's deputy. You were seen riding away from the scene of his killing. You'll hang for that; neither your youth nor your sex will save you.'

'I didn't kill him.'

'Then who did?'

'I don't know,' she said quietly, then, with more steel in her voice, added, 'But I do know that you were responsible for the hanging of Cal Tumbrel. You had no reason to do that and I'll see that you're punished for it.'

Currier and Willis exchanged concerned looks, each wondering how the woman knew the fate of the young lad they'd caught out on the prairie, wondering if she'd witnessed the events in that prairie gully. Then Willis remembered.

'Your army buddy,' he said to the sheriff.

'Tom Belman!'

Gary Hudson repeated the name. 'I remember him,' he added. 'We were discharged on the same day.'

Lou Currier ignored him. He spoke to the woman.

'How did Tom Belman get involved in this?'

Sally shook her head in denial that there had been any involvement.

This time it was Currier who struck her, not with the brutish power that Willis had used but with slaps delivered by both sides of his hand that jerked her head right then left.

'You're not in any position to play games. Tell us how you met him. Is he the one who sent you to spy on us?'

'Nobody sent me,' she said. 'I only met Mr Belman this morning at the ferry.'

'Then he was the one who told you. I suppose the lad told him he was meeting you at the ferry before he took the horse? Yes, that must have been why he insisted that the horse hadn't been stolen; the lad had probably agreed to leave it at the ferry where he could borrow another one from the ferryman that would get him back to Amarillo — '

'That's not important,' interrupted Willis. 'What we need to know is whether the soldier told anyone else.'

'I think we can depend upon him reporting it to the law across the river. The Rangers will investigate. We've got to go.'

'Have you completed the work in the barn?' Willis asked Gary Hudson.

'Almost. Just packing away the last bits of the press.'

'Good.'

'Do I tell everyone to pack their gear?'

'Two or three men can remain here to tend the livestock. Make it appear that we haven't abandoned the place, that we're expected back.'

'That won't fool anyone for long,' observed Currier.

'Long enough for we three to get out of Texas,' said Willis. He dismissed Gary Hudson with a wave of his arm.

'What do we do with her?' Lou Currier asked.

Andrew Willis's expression was cold as he regarded Sally Locke's reddened face. There was only one thing they could do with her: it was merely a question of where and when.

'Tie her up and put her in the hay shed until we're ready to leave. We'll leave her somewhere along the trail.'

Sally saw the look that passed between the men and knew that an important word had been omitted by Willis. That word was '*dead*'; along the trail they would leave her dead.

8

In appearance the bay gelding in Sam Dack's barn had the edge over its black companion. Its coat was sleek, its legs were long and it held its head high when the lantern was carried to its stall. It was the one that Sam recommended so Tom Belman slung his saddle on its back while he argued with its owner. Sam wanted to raise a force of townsmen strong enough to storm the farm but Tom was against it, fearing that such a tactic might put Sally in greater danger.

'If they are preparing to flee from the place they won't want to contend with a fractious prisoner. They've already shown that they are prepared to be ruthless; they might kill Sally at the first sign of interference by the townsfolk.'

'Then the two of us will tackle them on our own,' insisted Sam. 'I'm no stranger to battle and I can squint along a rifle barrel as well as any man. Besides, Sally Locke is my employer, it's my place to assist her when she's in trouble.'

'No,' Tom told him without sympathy. 'There's no job. Sally hinted at that simply to find out what you knew about Willis's activities.'

Sam wasn't troubled by that revelation, he wasn't even surprised by it; he was no longer young but that didn't mean he'd lost his marbles. He'd known that Ortega Point wasn't big enough to warrant its own newspaper, but whatever reason Sally Locke had had for flattering him, he was content to bask in it. It gave him something to crow about and flaunt at his friend, John Carter. Even a false boost to his ego deserved some reward.

'Besides,' he told Tom, 'she's a nice young lady. I don't want to see her come to any harm.'

'Nor do I,' Tom told him. 'If I can get her away from the farm undiscovered then you can attack it with everyone you can muster.'

'And if you can't?'

Tom shrugged, making it clear that failure would cost the lives of both him and Sally.

'If we're not back by dawn then I guess that you are in charge. I'd advise you to get a telegraph message off to the Rangers as soon as the office opens in the morning.' He climbed into the saddle.

'Perhaps it's the army you should call in,' he said, 'the counterfeit money has been transported over state lines so it's a federal affair.'

Sam rubbed his chin then shook his head.

'I think I'll stick to the Rangers. Blue uniforms are still not a welcome sight to the folk around here.'

Tom didn't argue; he pricked the bay with his spurs and rode out of town.

With only moonlight to guide the way, Tom was unable to proceed at anything more than a steady pace; however, the directions he'd been given were precise and he had no trouble in finding the farm. Undetected, he reached a clump of trees about two hundred yards from the house, which provided an observation point. Considering the lateness of the hour, there was a great deal of activity beyond the farm gates. He counted four lit lanterns in the house veranda and could see others at several places within the compound, not all of them stationary. Now and then he glimpsed movement: indistinct shapes interrupting the light from the lanterns, men, and perhaps animals, passing between the house and its numerous outbuildings.

One of those outbuildings, a large structure to the right of the house, captured Tom's attention; it seemed to be the focus of most of the activity. A yellow light showed around its open doorway, evidence of several lanterns within, which marked it as the major point of activity. A faint noise had reached him, the hammering of industrious men although whether their toil was of construction or destruction he couldn't ascertain. What he did know was that the moving lights, the torches guiding men around the compound, either came from or went to that building. Tom reasoned that if counterfeit money was being printed on the farm then that building was probably the place to look for it.

Searching for fake ten-dollar bills, though, wasn't his mission, nor was he interested in any other criminal activity with which Andrew Willis and Lou Currier were involved. He had come to find Sally Locke and get her away from this place before any harm befell her.

It occurred to him then that he should have brought along Sam's black horse, too. When he found Sally he would need another mount to get her clear of the area. Riding double, they had little hope of reaching Ortega Point without being caught and none at all of getting to the ferry crossing on the Canadian. Tom was annoyed: going off half-cocked was not his normal mode of behaviour. Even though he knew the young woman was in peril and prompt action was required, he ought to have given more consideration to his plan; a moment's thought at the outset could often make the difference between success and failure.

Mentally, he shook off the moment of self-censure; he would do whatever was necessary to rescue Sally.

Tom didn't know how many men were at the farm; he assumed there would be at least six in addition to Willis and Currier. Assessing the situation, he figured that Sally Locke was unlikely to be in the building that was the centre of most activity; most probably he'd find her in the house that was at the opposite side of the compound. Finding her without alerting everyone to his presence was his best hope of success. All he had to do, he told himself as he stealthily approached the farm on foot, was to avoid the moving lanterns and keep out of the glow of those that were stationary.

He was no more than twenty paces from the boundary fence when he caught the sound of footsteps and voices and realized that a guard had been stationed at the gate. Tom dropped to the ground, hoping that in the darkness the low-growing scrub would be sufficient to conceal him from the sight of those who manned the barrier ahead.

'What is it, Bill?' The question was uttered in a low voice but still it carried to where Tom lay, bringing with it a hint of anxiety in the speaker.

'Thought I saw something moving out there.'

There was silence for a few moments. Tom guessed the men were peering into the darkness, searching for an explanation.

'Coyote, I reckon,' the second man offered.

'Could be,' the first man agreed.

'Are we expecting trouble?'

'I'm not sure, but there has to be some reason for all the activity.'

'Are we clearing out?'

'You know as much as me, but Willis has a fast horse saddled and Lou arrived with a riding animal tied behind a buggy.'

'We should get our cut before they leave here.'

'Yeah! I expect Willis will let us know what's happening. Stay alert.'

Tom heard the scuffing of boots across the hard-earth ground as one man walked away. He waited as the sound diminished until it was lost among the other noises within the compound. He waited a few moments more while considering his next move.

It was clear that he couldn't remain in that place for long, nor could he make a direct beeline for the fence. The house, his primary target, was away to his left. By circling in that direction he might be able to find a place to breach the fence but he would have to proceed with the utmost caution. There might be other guards around the perimeter, although he thought it probable that only the main approach was being watched.

Moving slowly, squirming along the ground, availing himself of every scrap of cover provided by sagebrush and ground weeds, Tom put distance between himself and the man who remained at the gate. The fence was a triple row of poles, the gap between them wide enough for him to crawl through, which is what he did when he reached a point that would take him into the compound a few yards to the rear of the house. The greatest risk to discovery came in those yards close to the fence but he gambled that the guard at the gate had been posted to watch for riders approaching the farm and his attention would be fixed on the main trail. The possibility of running into other guards around the perimeter was a chance he had to take.

He reached the fence without challenge or being shot at. To keep as low as possible, he considered crawling under the bottom pole. That gap, however, was much smaller than those between the poles and crossing into the compound would take a few seconds longer. So he put his hands on the bottom pole, ducked his head and pushed his way under the middle pole.

From the moment when he put his hands on the bottom pole Tom was aware that something was wrong. Instead of affording a firm base from which to push himself beyond the barrier the timber sank under his weight; immediately Tom realized that it had been fractured and left unrepaired. No matter how quickly he might have reacted, it was too late to prevent the pole from breaking completely. The snap cracked loudly in his ears and, he supposed, was loud enough to alert everyone to his act of trespass.

He stumbled, fell, rolled and pulled his pistol from its holster. For a moment he lay still, wondering from which direction the first investigator would arrive but there was no shouting or any sound of running feet. Loud as the noise of cracking wood had sounded in his own ears, it had not been significant enough, it seemed, to interrupt all the activity on the farm. Tom stood, considered his surroundings and fixed on a course that would take him down the far side of the farmhouse.

Then a shout came out of the darkness from somewhere along the fence.

'What's happening?'

Tom looked in the direction of the gate. There was movement, someone coming towards him: the guard, he supposed, investigating the unexpected noise.

Tom moved swiftly, seeking the shadowed darkness of the building, pressing himself into the blackness, clutching the pistol and hoping he didn't have to use it and so reveal his position. He heard a door open at the front of the house; if those inside were also investigating the noise he was bound to be discovered. A water barrel offered a temporary hiding-place; there was just room for him to crouch behind it. It wasn't an ideal place to hide: he was, effectively, trapped between it and the house, but there was no alternative.

He squatted, held his breath and waited.

The guard came into view from the rear of the house just as two figures emerged from the front of the building. To Tom, there seemed something strange in the way they moved, awkwardly bumping together, like uncompanionable Fourth of July celebrants. He soon realized that a struggle was in progress: the slighter figure seemingly reluctant to go with the other but, with tied hands, finding it impossible to resist. That he had found Sally Locke afforded Tom no immediate cause for rejoicing. Until he could extricate himself from his own predicament he was in no position to rescue her. He wondered where they were going and how, if he lost sight of them, he would find her again.

The guard at the other end of the building advanced, sweeping his rifle before him.

'Hey, Cole,' he called, attracting the attention of Sally's captor, 'anybody passed you?'

Cole said he hadn't seen anyone and at the same time shook his recalcitrant prisoner in an effort to curb her attempt to escape his clutch by kicking at his shins.

'Thought I saw somebody,' the guard told him, but Cole wasn't interested in the other man's problems, he had enough trouble of his own with which to contend. The guard walked down the side of the building, gave the water barrel a questioning look as he passed but didn't stop. When he reached the end of the farmhouse wall he turned out of sight, to complete a full circuit of the building, which would take him back to his post at the gate.

Keeping to the shadow of the building, Tom moved quickly. On reaching the corner he peered round it to assure himself that the guard was no longer curious about the earlier sound he'd heard or the shape he thought he'd seen near the house. A veranda, inset twelve feet from each corner, was attached to the house frontage. A man was sitting on the rail smoking, the red tip of his cigarillo a bright spot in the dark night. He was looking at Tom, at first without concern, then with curiosity, finally with recognition.

'Belman,' he said, flipping the smoke clear of the timber building in a spinning arc.

Although surprised to find himself face to face with one of Willis's crew, Tom wasn't as slow to react as the man on the porch. He had no friends here, every man was an enemy. However, the other's slow manner had an effect on Tom, keeping him rooted to the spot while they looked at each other. For those few moments it seemed as though time stood still. Then, just as the man on the porch gradually realized Tom's identity, so, too, did it lodge in Tom's mind that he knew the man sitting on the rail. In that moment all doubts that he'd had regarding Sally Locke's suspicions cleared away. He'd listened to this man describing the art work he'd done for the Union, the copies of Confederate money he'd helped to produce in the Union's fight against the Southern states.

'Gary Hudson,' he muttered, then he lunged forward.

Neither man harboured a past grievance against the other; this enmity was born of the moment: current circumstances pitted one man against the other. A shout of warning had barely escaped from Hudson's mouth before Tom reached him, his left hand grabbing the rough material of the other's shirt to pull him off the rail. Gary Hudson had begun to rise, so, with his momentum taking him in the direction of the house, Tom's effort to silence him became a greater struggle.

For a while their battle for superiority was an all-consuming contest; Tom was trying to overpower his opponent to prevent the raising of a general alarm, while Gary Hudson's sole concern was to escape Tom's grip. Defeat was unthinkable to both combatants: if Gary won Tom would be hunted by every man within the compound and rescuing Sally Locke would be impossible; if Tom won then the counterfeit money scheme might be uncovered and Gary would be a wanted man all across the nation.

The veranda rail being between them, it was difficult for either man to gain command of the fight. With his left hand Tom gripped the other's shirt tightly and refused to release it despite Gary Hudson twisting and jerking to break free. A shout came from somewhere in the dark — the edgy gate guard, Tom suspected — returning to investigate the new disturbance. By the light of the lanterns hanging in the veranda the struggle would be visible to others.

Boosted by the prospect of an ally's assistance, Gary moved closer to Tom, hoping that the move would confuse his adversary, make him believe that he had given up the struggle of trying to break free. In fact, it was a ploy to enable him to swing a punch which might be enough to disable Tom until help arrived. It proved, however, to be Gary Hudson's undoing. Stepping closer not only brought Tom within range of his fists but it also brought him near enough for Tom to hit him, too, and Tom reacted most quickly.

Gary's movements were awkward as he tried to manoeuvre into a position from which he could generate leverage into a punch. A sudden tug on his shirt caused him to stumble and he was knocked further off balance when a boot heel sank in a gap between two boards. Grasping this advantage, Tom pulled at the man's shirt one more time, causing his opponent to lower his head. Tom hit it with great force with the pistol he held in his right hand. Gary grunted, sagged, then dropped unconscious on the boards when Tom hit him again.

Now there was no time to lose. The guard shouted again and Tom was well aware that if he remained in the lamplight he would be a sitting target. In addition, noises from within the house suggested that the attention of those inside had been aroused to the commotion on the porch. He turned and ran in the direction that Sally had been taken, keeping low, making himself a difficult target to hit. Nonetheless, a bullet whistled overhead as a gunshot crashed through the black night. Another followed but it came no closer to hitting Tom.

Men behind were shouting. Tom recognized Lou Currier's voice. He kept running. Ahead, two figures stood near a barn door, one much slighter than the other. As he approached them the bigger man threw a question, wanting to know the reason for the gunshots. The answer he received was supplied by the barrel of Tom's revolver crashing against the side of his head. As he collapsed, Tom gripped the young woman's arm; this, if it was intended to transmit a message of comfort, was a vain gesture. Even though they were no longer in a glow cast by lanterns, more bullets were being fired in their direction. Not only were they the targets of those in their wake, but men who had quit the large barn to investigate the shooting were being ordered to direct their fire at them.

A man carrying a lantern lit the way for the men from the barn. Tom shot him, heard his last startled cry as he pitched forward, The lantern shattered and its oil spread across the ground. For a brief moment a naked flame illuminated the legs of three men who had paused beside the body of their comrade.

'We can't wait here,' Tom said, casting his eyes around the compound in an effort to find an exit or a haven from which to stand off their oppressors.

Sally, wide-eyed, aware of the danger in which they found themselves, jerked her head towards the barn.

'There might be a way out at the rear. Perhaps we'll be able to escape that way.'

Though ignorant of the layout of the farm and handicapped by the dark night, Tom agreed it was worth a try. Two bullets crashed against the timbers as he hurried the girl inside the barn. Once inside, Tom withdrew his clasp knife and cut the bonds that tied Sally's wrists. Then he replaced the spent shell in his revolver; with only one gun between them he would need to take every chance that was presented to him to keep the chambers full. He knew their chances of escape were very low but he'd learned in the war that it was important to keep fighting and use any advantage that came your way.

Outside, a fusillade was fired at the building. Tom and Sally listened to the sound of the bullets striking the walls and door.

'The timbers are stout,' Tom observed. They were words of weak encouragement.

Sally's lips moved to form a weak smile that acknowledged his attempt to encourage her but at the same time dismissed the need to patronize. She was aware that they were in a difficult situation but what she couldn't fathom was his sudden appearance in this place. In her opinion, he had done enough to help her back at the ferry; if she'd heeded him then they wouldn't be facing death now. She didn't shrink from the prospect of death because there was little likelihood that they would get out of this barn alive. She watched as Tom Belman opened the door slightly to see what their besiegers were doing. Several shots forced him to close it quickly. In the darkness his voice carried to her, steady, almost unconcerned.

'Another way out, Sally. Can you explore while I hold the door?'

Sally busied herself with a lantern she'd found; when it was lit she held it high to examine their place of confinement. There were several sacks piled against one wall. When she felt them she confirmed her belief that they contained animal fodder because the rest of the barn was being used to store hay. Bundles of it were stacked high, almost touching the planks that formed the flooring of the loft above. But there was no other door. She had made another bad decision and now they were trapped.

Another volley of gunfire peppered the door; this time Tom fired two shots of his own before being forced to withdraw and close the door.

'Not even a false offer of amnesty if we surrender,' he said. 'They don't mean for us to leave here alive.'

Sally nodded, her face fell as she

accepted that truth.

'You shouldn't have come back,' she said. 'Why did you?'

'A promise I made to get you safely home.'

'Who did you promise?' she asked, puzzled.

'Myself, but on behalf of young Cal. Your safety was his last wish. I failed to save him so I reckoned I owed it to him to complete what he started.'

'Instead, my stubbornness has got you killed, too.'

'We're not dead yet,' he told her.

His optimism seemed misplaced and she quoted him to prove it.

'You said they don't mean to let us out of here alive.'

'They don't, but that doesn't mean they'll succeed. You've got to keep fighting and believing, Sally.' That had been his mantra during the war. Somehow, surprisingly, he'd survived battles against superior numbers when all had seemed lost. He couldn't explain why he'd lived when many comrades had died, all he knew was that he had come through the war with a determination always to end whatever task he'd chosen to undertake. He'd made a decision to get Sally Locke back to her family and he would do that or die in the attempt.

No shots had been fired for a minute or more. Tom knew the men outside might be reloading their weapons in preparation for a renewed onslaught but it was important to know as much about the enemy's strategy as possible. With Sally in a safe position, he eased the door slightly ajar, only wide enough to provide a small glimpse of the activity in the yard beyond. What he saw caused a sharp intake of breath. He could see naked flames, most men were carrying burning brands and Tom knew they weren't for illumination. Willis had given the order to burn down the barn knowing that its stock of hay would transform into an inferno in moments.

Tom aimed at one of the torchbearers and pulled the trigger. The man went down and a second man also took a bullet before answering shots forced Tom to close the door again. Volley after volley was fired at the building, Tom's handgun was no match for the arsenal of weaponry ranged against him. He replaced the two spent shells and waited with his gun pointed at the doors ready to repel any attempt to take the place by storm. No one came and eventually the attack petered out and silence once more filled the barn.

Five minutes passed, then they began to hear activity on all sides of the barn. A couple of minutes later Sally gripped Tom's sleeve and pointed to the place where the fodder sacks were stacked. Smoke was rising and the crackle of burning wood could be heard. Then they saw flames jumping from the opposite wall, the tongues licking out at the hay bales. The smell of kerosene began to penetrate and smoke curled upwards.

Tom hurried across to the door and pushed. It didn't open, a restraining bar had been inserted into the outside housing, locking them in, condemning them to the blaze. He could hear gunfire and although nothing seemed to be striking the doors it was a clear indication that even if he and Sally escaped the growing inferno they would be shown no mercy.

Now, the straw was burning with gathering ferocity. Sally was coughing, cupping her hands over her mouth and nose in an effort to filter the smoke from the air she inhaled. Tom holstered his gun: it was useless now. Even though those outside were still discharging their weapons he knew that there was little chance of shooting his way out of this situation. He put an arm around Sally's shoulders and drew her further towards the back of the barn.

By this time the flaming hay was providing more light than they had until now been afforded. The new brightness revealed a ladder propped against an opening into the loft and the possibility of there being another exit occurred to Tom. He guided Sally to the ladder and urged her to climb. He was aware that people could choke to death in smoke and also that people survived longer by breathing the cleaner air beneath. If they didn't get out of the building quickly they would either die from the smoke or burn to death in the fire.

During his drift into the West since the end of the war it had been necessary for Tom to turn his hand to many forms of employment. Although he wouldn't describe himself as a natural farmer, he'd worked on several farms and it wasn't uncommon for lofts to have doors, offering a possible route out of the building. He was aware, of course, that Willis and his men could have their guns trained on any upper opening, but a quick end from a speeding bullet might be a kinder death than choking on smoke or being burned alive. As he climbed behind the young woman he could still hear sporadic gunfire but most of the guns, it seemed, were now silent.

Because flames hadn't yet climbed as high as the loft, vision was limited and made more difficult because the smoke was being trapped by the high rafters and was curling back to fill the void.

'Can you see a door?' he asked Sally, but she had her eyes closed, trying to protect them from the irritation of heat and smoke. He held her arm, led her forward to the nearest wall, then worked his way along it, feeling the heat under his feet from the fire below and on his hand as he felt his way along. Sometimes, later, when remembering the event, he would attribute finding the upper doors to instinct and at other times to a mental alertness that enabled him to retain and convert knowledge to practical use. He never said it was luck. The luck came when he threw open the doors and felt the smoke-free air on his face. Below him men with guns, alerted by the crash of timber, looked up, but no one fired at them.

A grizzled old-timer hollered up.

'Hold there, Tom. Hold there a moment.' Then he was helping men to push a cart of straw as close as possible to the burning building and urging the young couple to jump. Sally's eyes were stinging and watering so that she could barely open them wide enough to see the landing target. Tom held her hand, told her to jump as far from the building as she was able. The luck that night was that they fell side by side into the straw-filled vehicle and didn't shatter their bones on the ground below.

9

When Sally had been hustled roughly from the house to be locked up in the hay shed, Lou Currier had turned his attention back to the money that was piled on the small desk in the middle of the room.

'I reckon our partnership ends tonight,' he said. 'Time to share out the money.'

Willis dismissed the suggestion, spread his arms wide as though there was no cause for alarm.

'We can start again in another town. There's still a lot more money to be made out of this scheme before we need to stop.' His nonchalance was an act, part of the character he'd grown into, a character who believed that the haul lying on his desk was not big enough for sharing with Lou Currier or anyone else.

187

'You can go where ever you choose,' Lou told him, 'but not with my share of the money.' His hand had never been far from the butt of his revolver and it was there now to stress the point of his argument. Andrew Willis uttered a small laugh.

'Why so suspicious, Lou? I'm not planning on running out with the money. If you think it's time to follow separate trails then that's what we'll do. When they've finished in the far barn every man will get his share.'

That was when the first sounds of a disturbance reached them from out on the veranda.

'What's going on?' Willis wanted to know. No sooner were those words out of his mouth than they heard a shout followed by a gunshot. Both men rushed outside, where they found Gary Hudson slumped against the porch rail and, in the yard, 'Kansas' Bill holding a smoking rifle. The latter was peering into the darkness as though still seeking a target to shoot at.

'What's the shooting?' Willis wanted to know.

'Somebody slugged Gary,' replied Bill. 'He ran off in that direction.'

'Who was it, Gary?' Lou Currier wanted to know, crouching at the side of the stricken one-time soldier.

'Tom Belman.' His reply was almost drowned out by the sound of gunfire over in the direction of the outbuildings.

'Your army buddy!' Willis scowled as he spoke, his voice carried anger. 'So he's been involved in this all along.'

'His involvement ends here,' vowed Lou. With Gary Hudson nursing his sore head, they hurried off in the direction of the gunshots.

'They're in the hay barn,' they were informed and Lou ordered the men to keep the fugitives pinned down by peppering the building with rifle fire.

During the next fifteen minutes, despite a bombardment of lead from their guns, Willis and his men achieved nothing more than the removal of a number of splinters from the barn's solid timbers. Furthermore, they took casualties, an event which always had a disheartening effect on a crew. So the decision was taken to burn down the building.

'There's nothing in there but hay and fodder,' Currier said. 'We have no need for it if we mean to abandon this place tonight.'

While the doors were being barred and the walls soaked with kerosene, Willis sidled away, back to the house and the money. This was his opportunity to fill the saddle-bags, mount up and ride clear of Texas. Lou Currier was organizing the cremation of the meddling girl and her friend and they would all be watching the burning barn until its timbers crashed to the ground.

It didn't quite work out as Andrew Willis expected. Lou Currier was quick to notice his absence and its significance was not lost on him. Flames were beginning to climb the barn walls and an occasional shot was still being fired at the burning building when Willis left the house with the full saddle-bags slung over his shoulder. Currier was waiting for him on the veranda.

'It's not what you think, Lou,' Willis said, trying to bluff his way out of the situation. 'Mount up,' he told him, indicating the black horse, which was tied to the back of the buggy. 'When we're away from this place we'll split the money.'

'What about the rest of the crew? They deserve their share. There wouldn't be a scheme without Gary Hudson.'

'We'll come across him again; he'll get his share then, but I think we should get away now. It's still possible that the Rangers will come looking for us.'

Those words had barely left his mouth before the sound of fast-travelling horses reached them. Because every man had become embroiled in the commotion there was no longer a guard at the gate to shout a warning. The fire was now beginning to spread light over the whole compound and by the light of the flickering flames, Willis and Currier were able to identify some of the horsemen who now lined the fence. They were men from Ortega Point being led by members of the town committee. Some of them had rifles in their hands to back up the words of their head man, who was yelling out an order for the shooting to stop.

In the darkness of the veranda, Willis and Currier remained unseen by the new arrivals. As they came through the gate the townspeople had their eyes on the burning building to their right. One or two shots were fired in the air to stamp their authority on the situation and the instruction to the crew to throw down their weapons was eventually obeyed, but not before an exchange of gunfire was necessary to quell the resistance of a couple of the farmhands.

At the height of that little battle Lou Currier was killed. The shouts of the townspeople had made it clear that they were looking for the young woman. It wasn't clear to him what reason they had for believing she had been brought to this place but they seemed certain of their quest. They would lynch him, he knew, when they learned of her fate. He wasn't prepared to face such a death. He would rather go down with his guns blazing. Let them shoot him if he was to die.

Andrew Willis saved the townspeople the trouble. Lou Currier's back was a target he'd long been waiting for. The sheriff had taken only four steps before a shot from Willis's pistol struck him in the back of the head. He fell face down on the hard ground and died there.

Taking advantage of the affray near the burning building, Andrew Willis threw the saddle-bags over the rump of the white horse, climbed into the saddle and rode away.

★ ★ ★

Sam Dack, ignoring Tom Belman's instructions, had informed the towns-people of the situation that was on their doorstep. His tale of counterfeit money, the hanging of Cal Tumbrel and the abduction of Sally Locke had been supported by the testimony of John Carter. Even so, they'd ridden out of Ortega Point unsure of their right to ride on to land belonging to Andrew Willis, but the flames and the gunfire that greeted them bolstered their belief in the old man's story.

The discovery of Lou Currier's body brought a grim reminder to Tom Belman. He remembered Captain Blayney who, it was believed, had been shot in the back by Currier. He wasn't a biblical man, but the phrase about a man reaping what he sowed filled his mind. More pressing, however, was the fate of Andrew Willis. It was Gary Hudson, no doubt hoping to gain a little clemency, who observed that the white horse had gone from the rail outside the house.

'He can't be too far ahead,' Tom said, and despite the protests of Sam Dack, Sally Locke and the head of Ortega Point's committee that he had no reason to put himself in more danger, he mounted the black horse that Lou Currier had brought from town and set off in pursuit. Perhaps it wasn't his responsibility to hunt down the leader of a counterfeit gang, but nor was it his way to leave a task uncompleted. Besides, Willis had tried to kill him and Sally and if he were allowed to run free would most likely try to kill other people in the future.

It was clear that Willis would head north, hoping to reach the ungoverned land beyond the Texas border. The territory was rough and, to Tom, strange, which in addition to the darkness of night made it impossible to travel quickly. Willis, however, had the same problems with which to contend. A couple of times Tom thought he caught a distant glimpse of white but he wasn't sure and realized that it could have been a trick of the mind, deceiving him into seeing what he wanted to see. He rode on through the night until, with the coming of dawn, there was light enough to see tracks on the ground.

He found Andrew Willis an hour later, resting against a boulder while the horse drank from small waterhole. Tom sat astride his mount looking down on Willis for more than thirty seconds before the criminal realized he was under observation. When he did, the surprise caused his whole body to jerk. Then he relaxed, his shoulders slumped, as though he had no more fight in him, as though thinking that he'd given his best but been caught by a better man.

'I'm taking you back,' Tom said.

'They'll hang me.'

'That's right.'

'There's a lot of money in those saddle-bags. Half of it is yours if you say you couldn't find me.'

Tom didn't reply straight away. He knew that the offer was as false as the body gestures.

'Throw your gun away, then stand up,' he said eventually.

'I haven't got a gun,' Willis said, twisting to show both thighs and the absence of a holster.

'You shot Lou. You've got a gun.'

Andrew Willis grinned. It made him look even more sly, less trustworthy.

'It's in the saddle-bags.'

Tom didn't believe him.

'OK if I stand up?'

Tom nodded but kept his eyes on the man while he pushed himself awkwardly on to his feet. He was doubled over, as though exhausted by the night ride, and made a show of blowing out his cheeks as though struggling for air. His left arm reached out for the support of a nearby boulder while he struggled to straighten up. Halfway upright he paused and closed his eyes, as though the effort was too much. His right hand rested on his stomach. He looked up and grinned again. Then his right hand grabbed for the gun that was tucked into the waistband of his trousers, under his jacket, and he began to pull it clear. Tom shot him three times, although the third bullet wasn't necessary. He loaded the body across the saddle of the white horse and led it back to Ortega Point.

★   ★   ★

Next day three men were approaching the ferry point as Sally Locke and Tom Belman disembarked on the far bank of the Canadian. By the time the pair had bidden farewell to Enrique Domingo, one of the men had put spur to horse to urge it swiftly down to the waterside. He was Sally's father, the other two men were Texas Rangers. The destination of all three was Ortega Point, he to find his daughter, they in response to a telegraph message that had announced the end of the counterfeit gang who had been sought by law officers across the nation.

'I reckon this is where we part trails,' Tom said to Sally after they'd told their story to the Rangers.

'You promised to see me safely home,' she said.

'I think you're safe enough with your father.'

'You could still come to Amarillo. Father would find a job for you.'

Tom shook his head. 'Sam Dack wanted me to become sheriff of Ortega Point, but I'd be as bad a newspaperman as I would be a lawman.'

'So you're going to California?'

'That's right. That was the plan when I started and I'll see it through, otherwise I'd always be wondering what I hadn't seen.'

'Perhaps you'll come back this way again,' she said.

'Perhaps.'

'Make sure you look us up if you do.'

Tom tipped his hat to acknowledge the young woman's invitation. With a flip of the reins he set his horse moving on with the mule plodding at its side, heading west to the far sierras.

We do hope that you have enjoyed reading this large print book.

Did you know that all of our titles are available for purchase?

We publish a wide range of high quality large print books including:
Romances, Mysteries, Classics
General Fiction
Non Fiction and Westerns

Special interest titles available in large print are:
The Little Oxford Dictionary
Music Book, Song Book
Hymn Book, Service Book

Also available from us courtesy of Oxford University Press:
Young Readers' Dictionary
(large print edition)
Young Readers' Thesaurus
(large print edition)

For further information or a free brochure, please contact us at:
Ulverscroft Large Print Books Ltd.,
The Green, Bradgate Road, Anstey,
Leicester, LE7 7FU, England.
Tel: (00 44) **0116 236 4325**
Fax: (00 44) **0116 234 0205**